The Magic

Gwyneth Rees is half Welsh and half English and grew up in Scotland. She went to Glasgow University and qualified as a doctor in 1990. She is a child and adolescent psychiatrist but has now stopped practising so that she can write full-time. She is the author of the best-selling Fairies series (*Fairy Dust*, *Fairy Treasure*, *Fairy Dreams*, *Fairy Gold*, *Fairy Rescue*, *Fairy Secrets*), *Cosmo and the Magic Sneeze*, *Cosmo and the Great Witch Escape*, *Cosmo and the Secret Spell* and *Mermaid Magic*, as well as several books for older readers. She lives in Middlesex with her husband, Robert, their daughters, Eliza and Lottie, and their two cats, Hattie and Magnus.

Visit www.gwynethrees.com

Also by Gwyneth Rees

Mermaid Magic

Fairy Dust
Fairy Treasure
Fairy Dreams
Fairy Gold
Fairy Rescue
Fairy Secrets

Cosmo and the Magic Sneeze
Cosmo and the Great Witch Escape
Cosmo and the Secret Spell

The Magical Book of Fairy Fun
More Magical Fairy Fun
Cosmo's Book of Spooky Fun

For older readers
The Mum Hunt
The Mum Detective
The Mum Mystery
My Mum's from Planet Pluto
The Making of May
Something Secret

Gwyneth Rees

The Magic Princess Dress

Illustrated by Jessie Eckel

MACMILLAN CHILDREN'S BOOKS

For Eliza and 'Bump',

with love

First published 2010 by Macmillan Children's Books
a division of Macmillan Publishers Limited
20 New Wharf Road, London N1 9RR
Basingstoke and Oxford
Associated companies throughout the world
www.panmacmillan.com

ISBN 978-0-330-46113-9

5 7 9 8 6

A CIP catalogue record for this book is available from
the British Library.

Printed and bound in the UK by CPI Mackays, Chatham ME5 8TD

1

It was Ava's mum who had suggested Ava take her fairytale book with her when she went to stay with her dad. Ava's mother had read to her from the book on many occasions and Ava always enjoyed listening to her animated voice bringing to life the entertaining – if unlikely – adventures of the various fairytale characters. Ava found the book extra-comforting now as she curled up on her bed at Dad's house to read her favourite story, about Cinderella. With any luck she would manage to forget for a little while that her mum was so far away.

Of all the storybook's heroines, Ava loved Cinderella the best. She wasn't sure why, but maybe it was because Cinderella seemed more believable at the start of *her* story than some of the other characters did at the starts of theirs. After all, in real life, nobody lived with seven dwarfs like Snow White – or

lived in a witch's tower, with hair as long as Rapunzel's. But losing your mother and having her replaced with a cruel stepmother and two horrible stepsisters was something Ava *could* imagine happening in real life. And because of that she always felt more drawn to Cinderella than to any of the other fairytale princesses. Of course the whole story became completely fanciful as soon as Cinderella's fairy godmother appeared and started waving her magic wand about, but by then Ava was always totally captivated. And time and time again she found herself being utterly charmed by Cinderella's magical transformation into the beautiful fairytale princess.

On this occasion, however, Ava found that she couldn't escape into the world of Cinderella as completely as she usually did. She couldn't seem to keep her mind on the story — and it wasn't just because she was missing Mum. The thing that was really bothering her was that Cindy, her cat, whom she had brought with her to Dad's house, had gone missing a few days earlier.

If only *I* had a fairy godmother who could magic Cindy back again, Ava thought, as she put down the book halfway through the story.

Her gaze fell on the little pile of CAT MISSING posters she had made using Dad's computer. There was a description of Cindy printed on each one, together with Ava's mobile-phone number and her dad's address in case anyone found her. Ava had already put up several posters on lamp posts in the streets around Dad's house.

Perhaps now would be a good time to go and see if she could put some up in the windows of the local village shops, she thought. After all, in *real* life there was no such thing as magic to help you out when you had a problem – and that meant that the only thing to do was to try and solve the problem for yourself.

She didn't bother to ask her dad – who was working in his study – if it was OK for her to go to the high street. Instead she wrote him a short note saying that she had gone out to look for Cindy, which she left on the kitchen table. It was Dad who had absent-mindedly left the back door open, letting Cindy escape into the garden. To make matters worse, Cindy's collar had fallen off – they had discovered it in the grass afterwards – so even if somebody had found her by now, they wouldn't know where she belonged. It had happened the day after Ava had arrived, and even though her dad obviously hadn't let Cindy out on purpose, Ava still felt angry with him. Both Ava and her mum had told him Cindy would have to be kept inside for the first few days to give her a chance to get used to her new environment – and he had promised he would be careful.

The trouble with Dad was that he never really listened to what you told him, thought Ava, as she left the house and set off towards the main street in the village. He was always thinking about something else, usually something to do with the books he

wrote – all about historical times.

Just as Ava was stopping to peer over
a wall into an overgrown front garden,
which was just the sort of hiding place
Cindy would like, her mobile phone started
ringing.

'Ava?' It was Dad and he sounded
worried. 'Where are you?'

'On that little side road that leads off
yours – the one that goes towards the high
street,' Ava told him. 'I thought I'd go and
see if any of the shops in the village will
put a poster of Cindy up in their windows.
Oh!' As she looked up she could see a small
corner shop a little further along the road.
'There's a shop on *this* street as well. Maybe I
can put one of my posters up in *its* window.'

There was a sharp intake of breath at the
other end.

'Dad, are you still there?'

'Yes. Listen. I want you to come home right now.'

'No, Dad,' Ava protested, 'I need to stick these leaflets about Cindy in as many shop windows as I can.'

'Ava, you are not to go into the shop on that street. Do you hear me?'

'But why?' Ava was surprised. Generally her father didn't seem to care what she did as long as she kept out of his way when he was busy working.

'Never mind why.' Dad's voice sounded unusually heated now. 'Just do as I say. Come home now and I'll help you with those leaflets later.'

'OK, OK . . .' she grumbled, nearly adding, 'Keep your hair on!' which was what she often said to Mum when she got into a flap unnecessarily about something. But she stopped herself because she wasn't sure how her dad would react if she were to tease him like that. She knew her mum so much better than her dad. After all, until this summer she had spent the whole nine years of her life living with Mum, only seeing her father two or three times a year for the occasional weekend. As she had pointed out to Mum on the way here in the car, Dad felt more like a distant relative than a father.

'Which is why it's great that you're going to stay with him this summer,' her mother had replied.

'I still wish you weren't going away for a whole six weeks,' Ava had said, frowning. 'I'm really going to miss you.'

'And I'll miss you, darling, but this sailing trip is something I've always dreamed of

9

doing. And your dad misses you too, you know. He wants to spend this time with you.'

'No he doesn't,' Ava had said crossly. 'All he has time for are those stupid history books he writes.'

'Ava, that's not true,' Mum had replied gently.

But Ava hadn't been sure if she believed her.

Now, as she slipped the phone back into her pocket, Ava couldn't understand why her father was making such a fuss. She had kept walking as she talked to him and she was already right outside the little corner shop – which looked like it sold second-hand clothes.

On the wooden board above the window

the name of the shop – MARIETTA'S –
was painted in large curly lettering, and
the window display consisted of a solitary
mannequin wearing a fuzzy blonde wig and
an extremely faded, hideously unfashionable
blue sequinned dress. From what Ava could
see through the dirty windowpane, the

11

clothing inside wasn't much better.

Ava was about to leave when she spotted a little card taped to the glass door just below the 'open' sign.

Printed on the card in large clear lettering were the words: *FEMALE TABBY CAT FOUND. ENQUIRE WITHIN.*

'Cindy!' Ava gasped, and totally forgetting everything else, she tried the door handle. The door opened at once setting off a little bell inside the shop.

Suddenly feeling sick in case the cat that had been found *wasn't* Cindy, Ava tried to stay calm as she looked around. She was standing in the small front section of the shop, which had a round clothes rack in the centre, full of the sort of second-hand clothes typically found in charity shops. Along one wall another rack was partly filled with dusty-looking old coats and jackets. The shop was half empty of stock, and what there was looked like it had been there for a very long time.

Oh, please let Cindy be here, Ava thought desperately.

In the centre of the back wall was a small archway, which presumably led through to the next room, but Ava wasn't sure if that room was also part of the shop or whether it was private. A multicoloured beaded curtain hung in the arch, preventing Ava from seeing through.

Ava was just wondering whether to call out to let whoever ran the shop know that she was there, when the curtain moved and a smiling young woman appeared.

The woman was slim with pale skin, green eyes and long, wavy, copper-coloured

hair that fell to her waist. She looked ten years or so younger than Ava's parents – in her late twenties maybe – and she wore a long flowing orange dress with big red flowers on it. Her sandals were also orange and she had a stunning necklace made of amber-coloured beads.

'Welcome,' the woman said, smiling at Ava cheerfully. 'I am Marietta. How can I help you?'

'I just read the notice in your window,' Ava mumbled shyly. 'I've

lost my cat and I think you might have found her.'

'Really?' The young woman was beaming now. 'What's your name?'

'Ava.'

'Ava! Such a pretty name! How long ago did you lose your cat, Ava?'

'It's been four days. My dad accidently let her out into the garden. I only just came to stay with him and I think she must have got lost. She's a tabby cat with a white bit on her front paw. Does the one you found have a white bit on her front paw?'

'Yes, I think she does.' And Marietta turned and disappeared through the beaded curtain without saying whether Ava should follow her or not.

Feeling curious, Ava followed as far as the archway before hesitating. She could hear

Marietta calling, 'Come here, puss! Oh . . . where *are* you? You were here a minute ago!'

'Maybe she'll come if *I* call her!' Ava suggested through the curtain.

'Of course! Come and help me look! I know she's here somewhere.'

So Ava pushed through the beaded partition and found herself in a very different room indeed.

'Wow!' she burst out, hardly able to believe that she was still in the same shop.

Marietta laughed. 'Do you like it?' she said. As Ava nodded enthusiastically Marietta added, 'I only let *special* customers get to see my *real* shop! First let's find your cat – then I'll show you round!'

2

The room Ava had stepped into seemed
like it belonged in another shop entirely.
Right in the centre there was a small gold
spiral staircase that led both upwards and
downwards. Another door – which was
closed – looked like it led even further back
inside the shop, and in one corner there was
a small changing cubicle with a gold sparkly
curtain pulled across the front.

The walls were beautifully painted
with scenes from fairytales – Rapunzel in
her white tower with her long gold plait
hanging down, a red-lipped Sleeping Beauty

lying on a massive four-poster bed, waiting for her prince to come and wake her up, and Prince Charming on a white horse holding a glass slipper on his way to find Cinderella.

Along one wall was a rail filled with exquisite-looking full-length dresses of every fabric, colour and design imaginable. Ava couldn't help staring at them in awe because each one looked fit for a princess to wear. A second wall had shelves from floor to ceiling, each shelf holding a different piece of fairytale costume. The top shelf had velvet hats trimmed with fur and cone-shaped hats with fancy ribbons or flowing scarves attached to the peaks. The shelf below had beautiful bonnets and pretty straw hats trimmed with ribbon. The next shelf down was stacked with different gold, bejewelled crowns and tiaras. Then came

a shelf filled with brightly coloured scarves
and another piled high with pairs of gloves –
black lacy ones, long white ones and
colourful silk ones. The two bottom shelves
contained nothing but footwear. There were
brightly coloured dancing shoes decorated
at the front with bows or silk flowers or

miniature fans, soft slippers with embroidery around the edge, little pointy-toed ankle boots made of shiny red leather, knee-length boots with fur trimming round the top, rainbow-coloured sandals that had little jewels set into the straps, and there was even a pair of solid gold flip-flops (which didn't look very floppy!).

Ava's gaze fell on Marietta, who was crawling on her hands and knees on the floor searching under the skirts of all the dresses, calling, 'Here, kitty!'

'Her name's Cindy,' Ava said, squatting down to help look. 'Are you sure she's in this room?'

'This was the last place I saw her, but I suppose she could have taken herself off into one of the other rooms by now.'

'How many other rooms have you got?'

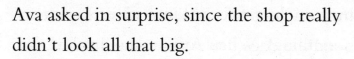

Ava asked in surprise, since the shop really didn't look all that big.

'Oh – I've lost count,' Marietta replied vaguely. 'It's a bit like a Tardis, this shop – much bigger on the inside than it seems from the outside.' She gave a strange sort of smile. 'Now . . . where can your little cat have gone? I haven't had any of the doors or windows open so she can't have escaped that way. Of course she might be hiding because she's trying to catch a mouse. There are an awful lot of mice in this building.'

Ava looked quickly around the floor, remembering what her mother had told her when she'd once asked how you could tell if a house had mice. 'I don't see any droppings anywhere,' she pointed out.

'Oh, the mice wouldn't come in here! This is my fairytale room – they'd be afraid they might get turned into white horses or something!' When Ava looked puzzled she added, 'You know – like in the story of Cinderella where the fairy godmother turns the pumpkin into a golden carriage and the mice into four white horses.'

Ava didn't know what to say to that, until Marietta smiled to show she had been joking. Ava smiled too then and said, 'It's an amazing shop. Where did you get all these beautiful clothes?'

'Oh, different places.' Marietta got to her feet and started to pull out some of the dresses to show Ava. 'I made these ones,' she said, showing Ava two dresses that were identical apart from one being pink and the other blue. They both had fitted bodices with high waists and long full skirts with underskirts beneath, and wide

sleeves trimmed with gold braid at the cuffs.

'You must be very clever,' Ava said. 'My mum can't sew to save her life, and she says she really envies people who can.'

'I use a special type of thread,' Marietta said. 'That helps a lot.'

'Really?' Ava waited to see if she was going to elaborate, but Marietta seemed to be finished with her explanation.

'Even my Barbie doll hasn't got dresses as beautiful as these,' Ava said as a particularly stunning gold dress with gold beads sewn into the skirt caught her eye. 'And she's a Barbie *princess*, so her clothes are *really* gorgeous!'

Marietta laughed.

Ava was just going to ask her who actually *bought* these dresses when they heard a faint miaow coming from above their heads.

'Cindy!' Ava gasped.

'Come on,' Marietta instructed, leading the way up the gold spiral staircase. 'She must have gone up to my fairytale-wedding section.'

'Fairytale wedding?' Ava queried.

'Yes. You aren't planning to be a bridesmaid any time soon, are you? If so then I've got just the right dress for you.'

Ava shook her head. 'I've never been to a wedding,' she said. 'Except my mum and dad's, but that was when I was a baby so I don't remember it. Mum says it was just a small wedding, which was just as well because they split up a year later.'

Marietta paused on her way up the stairs. 'It is very sad that your parents split up so soon. Do you still see both of them?'

'I live with my mum,' Ava explained, 'and I don't see Dad that often usually, but Mum's just gone away and left me with him for the whole of the school holidays.' She paused and added in a quieter voice, 'This will be the longest time Mum and I have ever been apart.'

'Are you missing her?' Marietta asked sympathetically.

Ava nodded, biting her lip.

'But now you and your father have the opportunity to get to know each other better,' Marietta continued brightly. 'That's a good thing, isn't it?'

'Maybe,' Ava said. Something about Marietta made Ava want to tell her more, and for a few seconds she totally forgot Cindy as she gushed, 'Though I'm not sure he *wants* to get to know me better. Mum's

25

tried to arrange for me to stay with him for longer before, but he's always been too busy. He spends half his time going off on long expeditions to places where he can do research for his books, and the rest of his time *writing* the books. Only I don't reckon any of them can be any good, because none of them are ever for sale in the shops whenever I go with Mum to have a look.'

Marietta looked thoughtful. 'What about you, Ava? Would *you* like to get to know *him* better?'

Ava frowned, thinking about her father, who always seemed so different from her friends' dads, and much more distant.

'Well . . . yes . . .' she admitted. 'The problem is, I'm just not sure *how*.'

'Oh, you'll find a way – don't worry about that,' Marietta said, smiling at Ava before continuing up the spiral stairs to the room above. 'Oh, gosh,' she blurted as she reached the top.

'Wow!' Ava gasped.

There were even more beautiful dresses in this room than there had been in the one below, but what really shocked Ava was the strange golden light bathing the room. It was as if a multitude of sunbeams were coming in from all different directions.

'What is it?' Ava whispered.

'It's a . . . well . . . a . . . a *thing* that happens here sometimes,' Marietta murmured, 'but I don't know how it can have –' She suddenly broke off as she noticed that one of the dresses on a nearby rack had slipped from its hanger on to the floor. She bent down to pick up the dress, which was a child-sized emerald-and-gold-coloured

bridesmaid's dress with a pretty beaded
bodice and a full skirt decorated with big
floppy gold bows. 'Look. One of the bows
has been pulled off,' she said, pointing at a
piece of loose gold thread on the skirt.

'Cindy is always playing with ribbons and
bits of string and things like that,' Ava said
excitedly. 'And those bows are quite *dangly*,
aren't they?' Forgetting all about the strange
golden light, which was fading now anyway,
she started to look around the room for her
cat.

Over by the window she saw a work-
table with a sewing machine on it, and she
went across to see if Cindy might be hiding
underneath. There was no sign of Cindy,
but lying open next to the sewing machine
was a rectangular music box. It was very
like a music box Ava had at home except

that the little plastic figure that twirled round inside hers was a ballerina, whereas this one was a fairytale princess. Hanging up on a stand next to the table was a not-quite-finished,

absolutely-to-die-for raspberry-coloured princess's dress with tiny rosebuds sewn on to it, that looked like it was meant for Cinderella herself.

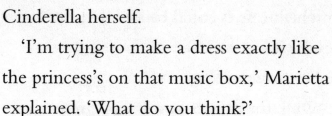

'I'm trying to make a dress exactly like the princess's on that music box,' Marietta explained. 'What do you think?'

'It's beautiful,' Ava murmured, briefly

29

touching the dress, which was made of the softest, silkiest material she'd ever encountered.

She went back to searching for Cindy, but after several minutes Marietta gently interrupted her.

'Ava, I don't think she's here any more,' she said, still holding the dress that the bow had been torn from.

'But she must be. We just heard her miaow, and I'm sure she pulled the bow off that dress!'

'I know. I can't find that bow and I think it might have got caught in one of her claws, in which case it could be said that she's now *wearing* it.'

Ava frowned. 'So?'

'Well, the dresses in my shop aren't the same as other dresses. Like I said before, they

are made with very special thread – *magic* thread in actual fact.'

Ava gaped at her, wondering if she had heard correctly.

'I know it must sound strange, but you see, the clothes in my shop give a certain magic power to certain people . . . and I'm guessing certain *animals* . . . who put them on,' Marietta continued solemnly.

Ava felt unexpectedly giggly. Marietta had a weird sense of humour – that was for sure. 'Do they make the people and animals invisible?' she joked. 'Like a magic cloak.'

'No, no . . . not invisible,' Marietta replied, completely serious. 'If worn by the right person – a *gifted* sort of person, you understand – it can allow that person to . . . well . . . travel in rather an unusual manner. I've never seen an animal do it before, but

I've heard that most cats – being such free spirits – are in possession of the gift too.'

Ava suddenly saw that Marietta wasn't joking. 'Look, I just want to find my cat,' she blurted, taking a couple of nervous steps backwards. 'If she's not here any more, then where *is* she?'

'That's what I'm trying to tell you! You saw how the room was bathed in golden light just now. Well, that was due to a magic portal opening up.'

'*Magic portal?*' Ava stared in amazement at Marietta because only that morning she had found some books on magic in her dad's bookcase. She had opened up one of them and found a whole chapter on magic portals. According to the book, a magic portal was a kind of invisible magic gateway that linked two parallel worlds – or two different time

32

periods within the *same* world. She had
found it strange that her dad owned such
books, but she hadn't yet had a chance to
ask him about them.

'That's right,' Marietta was continuing
calmly. 'I know it sounds hard to believe,
but many of the mirrors in my shop are
magic portals. To be able to travel through
one of them, a person who is *able* to travel –
and very few of us are, Ava – has simply to
look at his or her reflection in the correct
mirror – the mirror that is the right one
for the dress they have on – and the magic
reaction will begin. To stop the magic, you
simply have to turn away from the mirror
. . . it's quite within your control so there's
nothing to worry about . . . but of course
if you don't *want* to stop it, you must keep
looking until the light gets so bright that it

33

forces you to close your eyes. Then you will be transported through the portal.'

'But . . . but . . . that's just . . . it's . . . ridiculous!' Ava burst out.

Marietta shook her head, saying gently, 'I promise you, it's true, Ava. It must have been pure chance that made Cindy look at her reflection in the right mirror while she had the bow from this magic dress caught in her claw. And if you change into this dress, you'll be able to follow her.'

'*Follow* her?' Ava practically choked on the words as she found herself noticing for the first time just how many mirrors there were in this room. As well as several full-length ones, there were about a dozen different wall mirrors – round ones, square ones, oblong ones, oval ones and even a hexagonal one. They were all different sizes

and styles, some having antique frames while
others looked more modern. And they were
all gleaming at her invitingly.

'Yes,' Marietta said encouragingly, 'though
there is just one
thing that might be a
problem. You see, the
very *first* time a person
travels, they have to
choose the correct
mirror for themselves
or the reaction will
not happen. It's a way
of ensuring a person
is truly ready, I suppose. *I* was ready when I
was six years old – but for less . . . shall we
say . . . less *sensitive* individuals . . . it can take
much longer.' She smiled. 'I have a strong
feeling that *you* are ready, Ava, but there's

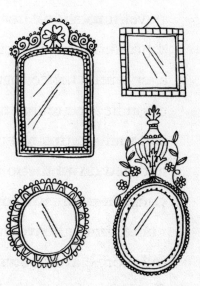

only one way to know for sure. You must put on this dress and then – with no help from me – you must try and choose the right mirror. If you are successful you can then travel through the magic portal to the place where your cat has gone.'

Ava felt as if her head was starting to spin. 'Stop it! You're scaring me!' she blurted. And without waiting for a response, she turned and fled down the spiral staircase, through the fairytale room and back through the beaded curtain into the front part of the shop.

For one awful, terrifying moment the front door didn't budge when she tried the handle, but then she tugged harder and it did. Half stepping, half falling out into the street, she slammed the door shut behind her. And she didn't look round as she ran as fast as she could back to her dad's.

3

By the time Ava reached Dad's street, she was beginning to think she had been silly to get so freaked out by what Marietta had told her. Marietta was a bit of a weirdo, that was all. Of course Ava couldn't deny that she had seen that strange golden light bathing the upstairs room – but there could easily be another explanation for it besides a cat travelling through a magic portal.

Dad had been very keen for her not to go into that shop and she wondered now if he knew about Marietta and her strange ways, and if he had been worried that Ava might get scared by her. If so, he hadn't been worrying for no reason, Ava thought, frowning. She *had* felt scared, and yet to start with Marietta had seemed totally charming. And the dresses in her shop were without a doubt the most beautiful gowns Ava had ever seen – including all the ones she had ever seen on television or in books.

As Ava let herself into the kitchen through the back door her father appeared immediately to greet her. 'At last!' he exclaimed. 'I've been trying to phone you and I was just about to go looking for you. What took you so long?' His thick dark eyebrows were bunched together in a worried frown and his shock of dark hair looked even bushier than usual – as if he had forgotten to even run his hands through it, let alone use a comb, when

he'd got out of bed that morning.

'Don't know,' Ava grunted, flushing because she knew that was a lie and she wasn't used to lying. She almost always told her mum the truth about things, but she found herself shrinking from telling Dad the truth about this. She just wasn't sure how he would react. Would he understand why she had gone into the shop if she told him about the card she had seen in the window?

'My phone's right here,' she added, slipping her hand into her jacket pocket for it. Her phone hadn't been ringing at all and she reckoned Dad had probably been using the wrong number. Dad was always scrawling down people's phone numbers in a careless manner and not being able to read his own writing afterwards. Since the phone wasn't in her right pocket she tried the left –

only to find that it wasn't there either. She frowned. Where was it?

'Ava, did you disobey me and go round the shops with those posters just now?' Dad asked sternly – and that's when she realized that she didn't have the posters either.

'Oh, no!' she gasped, remembering putting them down – along with her phone – on the counter in Marietta's shop before starting to look for Cindy.

'Oh no – *what*?' Dad demanded.

'I must have left them behind,' she mumbled.

'Left them behind *where*?'

She didn't see how she could avoid telling Dad the truth now – and she just hoped he wouldn't get too angry. 'I think I've left my phone and the posters in that little shop I told you about. I only went inside because they had a card in the window saying they'd found a tabby cat.'

'Ava!' Dad thundered. 'I expressly told you not to go into that shop!'

'I know, but you didn't say why, and . . . and anyway I *had* to when I found out Cindy might be inside. I really have to find her, Dad. Imagine how she must be feeling right now – all scared and lonely.'

'Ava, you know how sorry I am about letting Cindy out . . . but I really can't have you running about on your own in the village, going wherever you please,' Dad said crossly.

'That's not what you said the other day,' she reminded him defensively. 'The other day you said you thought it was terrible the way children don't have any freedom any more. And you said you didn't mind me going to the shops on my own as long as I'm careful.'

'Not to *that* shop!'

'Why not?'

He narrowed his eyes. 'Did you meet Marietta?'

'Yes – she showed me round.'

'She showed you round the *whole* shop?'

'Most of it, I think.' Ava was studying her dad's face closely. 'Dad, do *you* know Marietta? Have *you* been inside her shop?'

Her father immediately flushed – which wasn't like him at all – and instead of answering he asked, 'So what did you make of her?'

'She was really weird,' Ava began slowly. 'She told me she makes the dresses with magic thread and that the mirrors are magic portals.'

'She told you *that*?' Dad sounded outraged.

'Yes, but aren't *you* a bit into magic too, Dad?' Ava asked him quickly. 'I mean, why have you got all those books about it, if you're not?'

'What books?' he snapped.

'The ones on the bottom shelf in your bookcase. I saw them there this morning.'

Her father's face turned an even brighter red as he mumbled vaguely, 'Oh . . . yes . . . well . . . I happen to collect books on many different subjects, Ava. That doesn't mean I am *into* all of them, as you call it.'

'Well, do you *believe* in magic?' Ava asked curiously. 'In magic portals, for instance?'

'Ava, enough of this! As I'm sure you have discovered for yourself, Marietta is a very strange woman, and I don't want you spending any more time with her. Is that clear?'

43

'But—'

'IS THAT CLEAR?!'

Her father had never shouted at her like that before and Ava was shocked. She felt tears start up in her eyes.

'I wish Mum had taken me with her when she went sailing!' she burst out as she brushed past Dad, out of the kitchen and up the stairs to her room, where she slammed the door shut behind her.

Dad didn't come upstairs to try and comfort her – even though he must have guessed she was crying. It didn't really surprise her, since Dad never knew what to say when anyone cried.

Ava managed to comfort herself a little by sitting on her bed with her laptop balanced on her knees, writing an email to her mum.

44

She had already written to tell her about
Cindy escaping. Now she told her about
coming across Marietta's shop and about the
weird experience she had had there. She also
told Mum how much she was missing her
and how upset she was with Dad.

She had almost finished her email when she started to feel really thirsty – from crying such a lot, probably – so she decided to go down to the kitchen to get a drink.

She paused on her way down the stairs, hearing voices in the living room.

Her dad sounded cross as he said, 'You should never have shown her the back of the shop.'

A woman's voice replied impatiently, 'I *really* don't see what harm can come of it, Otto.' It was Marietta! And she knew Dad's name!

'You haven't got any children, Marietta, so you can't understand,' Dad snapped.

Ava hurried down the rest of the stairs and entered the living room. 'Understand *what*?' she demanded.

Her father jumped. 'Ava! I thought

you were in your room.'

'I was. I was writing an email to Mum.'
She turned to Marietta and asked bluntly,
'What are *you* doing here?'

If she had been that rude to a guest in
front of her mum she would have got into
trouble. But her dad didn't say anything –
probably because he wasn't that hot on
manners himself – and Marietta just smiled
as if Ava had given a perfectly friendly
greeting.

'Hello, Ava. I'm sorry if I scared you
before,' she said.

Ava didn't respond to that. Instead she
asked, 'How do you know my dad?'

'Oh . . . well . . . you see . . . your father
and I are—'

'Friends!' Ava's father put in before
Marietta could finish. 'We are all friends

47 ❀✿✾

with each other in this village, Ava. It's small enough to get to know everybody – not like when you live in the city.'

Marietta was giving Ava's father a strange look, and Ava frowned because Dad hadn't *sounded* as though Marietta was his friend when he had called her 'a very strange woman' earlier. But Ava was quickly distracted by another thought. 'Have you found my cat yet?' she asked, suddenly feeling hopeful that that might be the reason Marietta was here.

Marietta shook her head and pointed to the coffee table where Ava's mobile phone and the bundle of Cat Missing posters were sitting. 'I came to have a word with your dad and to return those. You know, you really shouldn't put your address on the leaflets, Ava. You could get any dodgy person turning up on your doorstep claiming to know where your cat is.'

Ava nearly asked what could be more dodgy than Marietta claiming that Cindy had disappeared through a magic portal into a parallel world. But she just managed to stop herself.

Marietta seemed about to say something else when Dad grunted, 'I've put a sandwich out for you on the table, Ava. You'd better go and eat it.'

'But—'

'*Now*, please, Ava.' Ava's dad could sound very stern sometimes and at those times she rarely had the nerve to argue with him.

As Ava took herself through to the kitchen she could hear her father showing Marietta out through the front door.

He came into the kitchen as she was

49 ❀❀❀

picking a piece of tomato out of her sandwich. (Dad never remembered that Ava didn't like tomatoes.) 'Have you actually sent that email to your mother?' he asked.

'Not yet,' she replied, looking up at him coolly.

'Did you tell her about Marietta's shop?'

Ava nodded, noticing that he seemed quite agitated.

'Do you think that's wise, Ava? Your mother will only worry – and we don't want to ruin her time away, do we?'

Ava hadn't thought of that. It was true that Mum probably *would* worry when she got Ava's email. But Dad seemed unusually

het-up, and Ava couldn't help thinking
that there was more to his anxiety than just
a desire for Mum to have a trouble-free
holiday.

'I'll delete the bit about the shop before I
send it,' she offered.

'Good,' Dad said, sounding hugely
relieved.

And Ava was certain then that her dad
had his *own* reasons for wanting to keep
Marietta's shop a secret. But what were
they?

4

Two days later Cindy still hadn't come back and Ava found herself thinking more and more about Marietta's shop. Strangely, her father's books on magic had been removed from his bookcase, and when she asked him where they were he told her they were antique books and he didn't want her sticky fingers all over them.

'My fingers *aren't* sticky,' she had snapped at him indignantly, but her father had just ignored her.

He had spent most of the last two days in his study, working on his latest history book.

When Ava had asked him what it was about he had told her he was researching the life of children in Victorian times.

Ava had learned a little about this at school. 'In Victorian times I'd probably have had a nanny, wouldn't I?' she had said.

'Maybe – if we were rich enough,' Dad had replied. 'If we weren't, you'd have been working in a factory or sweeping chimneys.'

'I thought chimney sweeps were all boys,' Ava had said, surprised.

'Sometimes they used girls as well,' Dad had told her, shuddering as if he was remembering something horrible that he had seen with his own eyes. 'They were cruel times. Just be glad *you* didn't live in them.' And he had cut short any further conversation by announcing that he had a lot of work to do and that he needed to get on with it.

Since it was now a lovely sunny afternoon – and Dad was busy in his study yet *again* – Ava decided to go out for a walk by herself and have another look for her missing cat. Dad had already warned her not to assume that the cat in Marietta's shop had *definitely* been Cindy. After all, since Ava had only heard a miaow rather than actually *seen* the cat for herself, how could she be certain? It was important to keep searching for Cindy closer to home, Dad said.

Ava could see the logic in his argument and when she got outside she tried to imagine that *she* was a cat who had just found itself in unfamiliar territory. Where would she go once she had left the garden? A cat would just follow its instinct, she thought.

She allowed herself to do the same, even though letting herself be guided by a *feeling* about where she should go wasn't something that she was very used to doing.

Maybe it was instinct or maybe it wasn't, but she was soon walking in exactly the same direction she had taken two days previously – and it therefore wasn't long before she found herself standing outside Marietta's shop. The card about the cat was gone today and the 'closed' sign was on the door. Nevertheless, she was sure if she rang the bell, Marietta would answer.

She had been waiting several minutes when an upstairs window opened and Marietta's head appeared. 'Oh . . . it's you, Ava! Just a moment. I'll come down.'

Marietta soon arrived on the other side of the door and drew back the bolt. The front room of the shop seemed just as drab and uninviting as it had done previously and it would be impossible to guess what the shop was really like on the other side of the beaded curtain, Ava thought.

'How are you, Ava?' Marietta asked as she invited her inside.

'OK, thanks – but I still haven't found Cindy.'

'If she's gone through one of my magic mirrors, there's no point in looking for her *here* any more,' Marietta said matter-of-factly.

'But we don't know for sure if that cat *was* Cindy,' Ava pointed out. 'It might not have been.' (She decided it was best not to question the authenticity of the magic mirrors again since Marietta clearly believed in them so passionately.)

'I suppose that's true,' Marietta admitted. 'Though I have a very strong *feeling* that it was Cindy. Don't you?'

Ava frowned. 'I don't know,' she said, wanting to add that in any case a strong feeling didn't amount to a fact. But she decided to keep quiet about that too.

'Well, in any case, I'm very glad you've come back because I don't think I made things totally clear to you the other day,' Marietta continued cheerfully. 'Of course, it's quite natural to feel sceptical – frightened even – when you first get told about the magic portals. Especially when nobody has introduced you to the idea of magic until now. But if you can just experience one of my portals for yourself, you'll understand everything. I should have explained to you that there's no need to be scared of going

to find your cat. You see, since the dress
with the missing bow – which your cat
took with it through the mirror – is from
my *fairytale* collection, then we know she
must have been transported to *fairytale* land.
There are many different fairytale lands,
you understand, but we have access to a
particularly nice one in this shop. And it's
a lovely *safe* place for you to visit if you
want to follow Cindy. All you have to do
is choose the right mirror in order to get
there – but that's easy too. There's only one
mirror in this shop that is the true gateway
to fairytale land. I'm sure you'll have no
trouble finding it.'

Ava knew she should have felt as
disbelieving and dismissive as she had done
on her previous visit to the shop, but for
some reason she felt different today. She

had a strange, excited feeling inside, as if lots
of fizzy bubbles had been let off inside her
tummy. Her sensible mind told her that no
one could travel through a magic mirror
into another land, but her imagination
decided to go along with what Marietta was
saying – at least for a little while. After all,
what was the worst thing that could happen?

'You won't tell my dad I was here, will
you?' Ava checked quickly.

'Don't worry, I won't *need* to tell him
anything,' Marietta said, smiling.

Ava thought it was a strange way of
answering but she guessed it was the best she
was going to get.

'Listen, Ava, we can talk about your dad
later,' Marietta added briskly. 'Right now
we must get on with preparing you for your
visit through the mirror. First you must

come and change into that dress. Follow me.'

Ava felt a tingly feeling run through her as she followed Marietta through the beaded curtain into the back room, where Marietta directed her to the changing cubicle. When she pushed back the gold sparkly curtain from the front of the cubicle, she found that the walls inside were a shimmery mother-of-pearl colour. There was a long mirror on one wall, and she briefly wondered if *that* could be a magic one – but it was so plain and ordinary-looking that she quickly dismissed that idea. The gold and emerald coloured bridesmaid's dress was hanging inside, waiting for her to change into. To her amazement it was exactly the right size, and she loved the way the bodice fitted snugly while the ankle-length skirt billowed out at the bottom. As well as fitting her perfectly, the colours seemed just right for her, somehow making her blonde hair look even blonder and her green eyes even greener.

'I look just like a fairytale princess!' Ava exclaimed, when she came out of the cubicle to show Marietta.

Marietta beamed. 'And that is what you shall be when you cross to the other side of the mirror,' she told her.

'I hope you're right,' Ava said, starting to giggle, because whatever else happened, dressing up like this was the most fun she'd had in ages.

'All you need now is some sort of decoration for your hair and some matching shoes,' Marietta said. 'Go to my accessories shelves and choose what you want.'

So Ava went over to the shelves she had spotted on her previous visit and chose a pair of emerald shoes with little gold bows on the front that seemed to have been made to match her dress. 'I can't believe they fit so well,' she said when she tried them on.

'It's just like when Cinderella tried on the glass slipper, isn't it?' Marietta said, with a twinkle in her eye.

Ava grinned, imagining herself as Cinderella offering her foot to the handsome prince. 'Do you think it would be too much to wear a tiara in my hair as well?' she asked

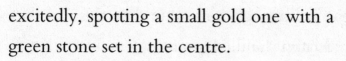

excitedly, spotting a small gold one with a green stone set in the centre.

'I don't see why not. You're a princess now, after all,' Marietta replied.

So Ava put on the tiara.

'Now,' said Marietta, 'it's time for you to choose which mirror is the doorway to fairytale land.'

'Do *you* know which one it is?' Ava asked, feeling as if she was taking part in some sort of thrilling party game.

'Of course, but I can't tell you,' Marietta said. 'Like I explained before, the wearer of the dress must find the mirror for themselves if the magic is to work the very first time they try it.'

'I think the mirror that belongs with this dress must be upstairs . . .' Ava began slowly. 'Because it was *that* room that had the golden light the other day . . .'

Marietta smiled, pointing encouragingly to
the gold spiral staircase. 'You know the way.'

So Ava mounted the twisting staircase for
the second time, taking care not to trip on
her long gown. At the top she paused and
looked around. The room hadn't changed
since her last visit. The work-table with the
sewing machine was still against the wall
under the window, and the rest of the room
was crammed full with rail upon rail of
beautiful wedding and bridesmaids' dresses.

Ava made up her mind to inspect each
mirror before she made her decision. The
first was a large oval one with a heavy
wooden frame. It looked old but nothing
about it reminded Ava of a fairytale. The
next two were rectangular with pastel-
coloured plastic frames – Ava was sure it

couldn't be either of them. The fairytale
mirror must be one of a kind, she thought.
On the end wall was a huge square mirror
with a very thick gold-painted frame that
had gold ivy leaves set into all four corners.
It was grand enough to belong in a princess's
palace, Ava thought, but somehow she
didn't think that was the one either. Then
she came across a small mirror with a
wooden frame that had animals carved into
it. There were birds, a family of deer, a
hedgehog and some very cute rabbits. Ava
really liked that one, but she still didn't think
it was the one she was looking for.

She began to check out the full-length
mirrors. The first was a plain oblong one
with a wooden frame that swivelled on its
wooden base. The next was similar except
that the glass around the edge had little

coloured flowers on it. Then, half hidden behind a row of bridesmaids' dresses, Ava found a mirror made from stained glass that seemed to contain all the colours of the rainbow. It was the most beautiful of all.

Ava gathered up her courage and stared into the mirror, trying to remember what Marietta had told her about the magic reaction. She stepped forward so that her face was almost touching the mirror, feeling excited as she waited to see what would happen next. Would she really be able to pass through the mirror to the other side? She took a deep breath and another step forward, but all that happened was that she bumped her nose against the glass.

She instantly felt silly – and angry with herself for being taken in by Marietta – and she was about to give up and tell Marietta

that the whole idea was
stupid, when her eyes
fell on the music box
that had been here on
her last visit. It was still
sitting on the work-
table next to the sewing
machine, but its lid was
now closed rather than
open. The picture on the lid was a very
pretty one of Cinderella wearing a raspberry-
coloured dress and a sparkling tiara. Slowly
Ava reached out and opened the box. It
immediately started playing a cheerful
melody, while the little princess figure inside
twirled round, just like the ballerina in Ava's
music box did at home. And just like the
dancing figure in Ava's music box, this one
was reflected in a small rectangular mirror on

the inside of the music-box lid.

As Ava stared at the little dancing princess she found herself remembering how Cindy – who was a very playful cat – sometimes sat in front of her own music box and gave the little ballerina a tap with her paw as it twirled round on its bouncy spring.

Carefully Ava bent down to look at the little mirror more closely. It was so small that she could only see her face and hair and the tiara on top of her head. But as she continued to gaze into the glass, something strange started to happen. The twirling Cinderella's reflection began to glow brighter and brighter. Then Ava saw that her own face had a yellow glow to it and that her tiara was getting more and more dazzling. Finally she found that she couldn't look into the mirror at all any more because

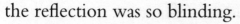

the reflection was so blinding.

After several seconds of keeping her eyes shut against the glare, the brightness seemed to lessen and Ava cautiously opened them again. The little rectangular mirror was still showing her reflection, but incredibly the music box within which it was set had completely changed. The box Ava was staring at now looked as if it had been hand-carved from a very fine goldish wood, and the whole thing was decorated with beautiful hand-painted multicoloured songbirds. Strangest of all, the little dancing princess figure now looked as if she was made of solid gold.

Ava gasped in shock and jumped back from the music box, turning breathlessly to ask Marietta what had just happened. But as she looked round she got an even greater surprise – for she was no longer in the dress shop!

69

5

Ava rubbed her eyes, hardly able to believe it. Instead of being in Marietta's shop, she was inside the most magnificent room she had ever seen — a room that looked like it belonged in a fairytale palace!

The room was huge, with massive windows framed by very grand gold and green curtains. The walls were also gold and on them hung several old-fashioned paintings and ornate mirrors. Ava looked above her head and saw that the high ceiling had beautiful cornicing around the outside and a dome in the middle with winged cherubs painted on it. A magnificent crystal chandelier was hanging down from the centre of the dome.

The furniture in the room was also very impressive. An enormous grand piano sat in the centre of the floor along with two huge gold harps. Several velvet-covered chairs, and couches with beautifully carved legs, were positioned against the walls, all of them scattered with richly coloured silk cushions. On various little tables around the room stood expensive-looking china ornaments and crystal vases containing beautiful scented flowers.

Ava looked down at her gold and green dress, which was the only thing that seemed to have remained unchanged. Her appearance was now perfectly in keeping with her new surroundings, she realized.

Ava barely had time to take in all of this, before a shrill voice behind her asked, 'Who are *you*?'

A second, equally snooty voice added, 'And who gave *you* permission to enter the palace music room?'

Ava whirled round to see, standing in the doorway, two girls in their late teens dressed in very expensive-looking

gowns. One was blonde, the other dark-haired, and they both had similar sharp features and scowling faces.

'W-where *am* I exactly?' Ava asked, hearing her own voice but feeling as if someone else was speaking the words.

'We just told you. You're in the royal music room. Only family members and special guests are allowed in here.'

'Yes,' said the other girl haughtily. 'So you'd better go back to the guest quarters with all the other princesses.'

Ava blinked. 'Princesses?' Maybe I'm dreaming all this, she thought.

The blonde girl was frowning. 'Well, *aren't* you a princess?'

'She must be,' said the other dismissively, as if princesses were two-a-penny. '*All* the bridesmaids are princesses. And she's

73 ❀❀❀

definitely a bridesmaid or why would she be wearing that dress?'

'Aren't you supposed to be at the rehearsal, or whatever it's called, with all the other bridesmaids?' the blonde girl asked Ava impatiently.

'I . . . I don't know . . .' Ava murmured, flushing. 'I came in here to look for my cat,' she added in a rush. 'You haven't seen her, have you? She's a tabby cat called Cindy.'

'*Cindy?*' The dark-haired girl started to laugh in a mocking sort of way.

'What is it? What's so funny?' Ava asked uncertainly.

'Did you *deliberately* call your cat after our sister?' the girl eventually spluttered. 'You really shouldn't have, you know – our sister is nothing like a cat!'

'No, she's nowhere near as clever,' the

blonde one added spitefully. 'For one thing, she's totally hopeless at catching mice! We used to lock her in the cellar at home and tell her she must catch at least one and wring its neck before we'd let her out again – but she never could!'

'She doesn't like to harm any animal – even a mouse – so we used to make her spend all day in that cellar,' the dark one added. 'Served her right for being such a goody-goody!'

'Such a pity she wasn't shut in the cellar when the prince came by with that silly glass shoe,' the blonde one said crossly.

'I know – and I never did understand why that shoe didn't disappear at midnight along with the rest of that interfering fairy godmother's trickery.'

'Wait a minute . . .' Ava could hardly

believe her ears. 'Is your sister *Cinderella*?'

'Of course,' snorted the blonde one. 'Who else did you think we were talking about?'

'Actually, she's our stepsister,' added the dark one. 'We are not truly related to her, thank goodness. Our dear mother married Cinderella's extremely pathetic father, who soon realized our mother was nowhere near as soppily gentle as his first wife. Soon afterwards he died, and after that it didn't take us long to turn that silly daughter of his into our servant. I am Ermentrude and this is my sister Astrid.'

'The *ugly* sisters!' Ava blurted out excitedly.

As soon as she'd said it she regretted her mistake. Both sisters' eyes flashed menacingly.

'Who do you think you're calling ugly,

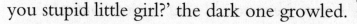

you stupid little girl?' the dark one growled.

The other sister took a few steps closer
and hissed in a threatening voice, 'Perhaps
you'd like to tell us exactly which princess
you are before we throw you into the palace
dungeons?'

Ava felt her mouth go dry. Panicking,
she did the only thing she could think of.
She turned her back on them and stared as
hard as she could into the little mirror in
the music-box lid, wishing desperately to be
transported back to Marietta's shop.

In a matter of seconds the gold dancing
figure began to glow brightly, and soon
Ava's face in the mirror was glowing too. As
the two ugly sisters came further towards her,
Ava closed her eyes – and she didn't open
them again until the bright light had gone.

Ava could feel her heart racing as she

allowed her wobbly legs to lower her trembling body on to the floor, where she sat gradually getting her breath back. She was in Marietta's shop again, in the room at the top of the spiral staircase and she could hardly believe what had just happened to her.

Marietta wasn't crazy after all! The magic was real!

There could be no logical explanation for what had just happened. She didn't even try to think of one. Her mind felt temporarily frozen, as if there was no point in trying to think at all any more. She felt as if all her previous thoughts counted for nothing after what she had just discovered.

As she sat there slowly recovering from the shock, she became aware of Marietta's soft voice in conversation with

someone in the room below.

'You shouldn't try to stop her, Otto. It's not natural. She has the same gift as you and me and she should be allowed to use it.' Marietta was talking to her dad! He must have discovered she was gone and come looking for her.

Ava heard her father's voice then, low and angry. 'Just because she's *able* to do a thing, doesn't mean she *has* to do it,' he said. 'Now where is she?'

Ava couldn't believe what she was hearing. Her dad clearly knew all about the magic mirrors – and about Ava's ability to use them. And what's more, it sounded as though he might be able to use them himself!

'What makes you think she's still here?' Marietta was asking him.

'She'd better be,' Dad said sharply.

'Well, she isn't.' Marietta sounded defiant. 'She's gone travelling!'

'I don't believe she's gone through a mirror already,' Dad snapped. 'She wouldn't be that reckless.'

She could hear her father stomping about angrily downstairs after that, searching for her. Any minute now he would come up the spiral stairs and find her, and then she would be in big trouble for disobeying him. Not only that, but she was sure he would forbid her from using the magic mirrors again – and then how was she ever going to find Cindy.

She looked at the music box, still open on the table.

As she heard her father opening and closing more doors downstairs, Ava knew what she had to do if she wanted to avoid being

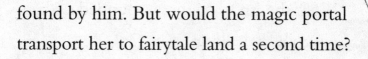

found by him. But would the magic portal transport her to fairytale land a second time?

As soon as she looked into the mirror, the light began to glow. Holding her breath, she closed her eyes, keeping them closed until the bright light had passed – and when she looked again she found, to her relief, that not only was she back in the palace music room, but that the room was empty.

It wasn't empty for long however. Just as Ava was starting to look around for Cindy, an older lady in a plain blue gown came sweeping in through the door. She was followed by five pretty girls who all wore bridesmaids' dresses identical to Ava's. Each girl had her hair piled up on her head and wore either a small crown or a tiara and Ava was certain they must all be princesses.

The ugly sisters were nowhere to be seen, thank goodness.

The older woman (who Ava guessed was some sort of governess) stopped when she saw Ava. 'Our sixth bridesmaid. Excellent!' She walked past Ava to the piano. 'As you can see, girls, here we have some music to practise with.'

'What are we practising?' Ava asked the

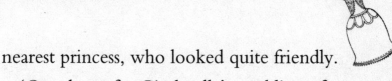

nearest princess, who looked quite friendly.

'Our dance for Cinderella's wedding of
course,' the girl replied. 'This is our dress
rehearsal.'

'Really?' Ava's head felt spinny with
sudden excitement. She could hardly believe
that she had arrived in a place where not
only was she one of Cinderella's bridesmaids – but she would actually be dancing
at her wedding!

The friendly princess giggled as she added,
'You'll never guess who we just met in
the corridor. Astrid and Ermentrude! They
looked really pale. They said there's a ghost
in here – a vanishing ghost who looks like a
bridesmaid!'

Ava gulped as all the bridesmaids started
giggling.

The older woman clapped her hands for

silence. 'I pity *any* ghost who is unfortunate enough to meet those two on its travels,' she said briskly. 'They may be Cinderella's sisters, but they are two of the rudest, most unpleasant, most *hysterical* creatures I have ever met. Now come on, girls . . . Let's move some of this furniture out of the way so that we have room to practise.'

As the princesses started to move chairs and tables to the edge of the room to clear a space to dance, Ava asked them, 'Have any of you seen a little tabby cat with a white patch on her front paw? She's my pet and she's gone missing.'

'A cat as a pet!' one of the princesses exclaimed. 'What a strange thing!' She looked down at the skirt of Ava's dress and added a little snootily, 'Do you know there's a bow missing from your gown?'

'Yes,' Ava replied apologetically. 'I think my cat has it.'

All the princesses started to giggle again then, until the older woman clapped her hands together a second time. Looking sternly at Ava, she said, 'Your Highness, no princess with a less than perfect gown may attend Cinderella's wedding. You must visit the palace seamstress without delay. There is a servant just outside the door and I'm sure he will show you the way.'

Realizing she had been dismissed, Ava headed curiously for the door. She stepped out into a corridor with a plush red carpet and royal portraits hanging on the walls, and immediately saw the servant. He was standing very still, staring straight ahead and wearing smart knee-length breeches, a tight jacket with long tails and a white powdered wig.

'Excuse me,' Ava asked him politely. 'Have you seen a tabby cat anywhere? She might have a gold bow caught in one of her paws.'

The servant looked down at her as if he suspected she was making fun of him. 'There are dozens of cats in the palace grounds, Your Highness, though I have not, as yet, seen one with a bow.' He gave her a cool stare as he added, 'Will that be all?'

'Yes . . . I mean, no . . . Could you please show me the way to the palace seamstress?' she blurted.

'Follow me, Your Highness,' the servant replied in a haughty voice. And he led the way along the corridor, down a flight of spiral stairs, along another corridor, up

two further flights of stairs and along yet
another corridor until he came to a halt
outside a plain wooden door.

'The palace seamstress is within,' he
declared, knocking on the door. Without
waiting for a reply he swung open the door
and stood with his back against it so that Ava
could enter. 'Your name, Your Highness?'
he asked her.

'It's Ava – but you don't have to—' she
began, only to be interrupted by the man's
booming proclamation.

'Her Royal Highness, the Princess Ava!'
he bellowed.

A young servant girl, with big dark eyes
and a single plait that fell halfway down
her back, immediately jumped up from
her stool and curtsied. She looked a few
years older than Ava – twelve or thirteen

maybe. Behind her a small elderly lady, with wrinkled skin and grey hair done in a bun, who was sitting in a chair by the window, put down her needle and thread and struggled to her feet to do the same.

Ava felt embarrassed and very guilty about an old lady curtsying to her like that. 'Please sit down,' she said as the manservant left them.

'*You* must sit first, Your Highness,' the old woman said. 'Here. Take my chair. It is the most comfortable.'

'No, thank you,' Ava insisted. She quickly dropped to the ground, where she sat cross-legged as if she was in her school assembly hall. From there she looked around the

※❀❁ 88

small room, which was filled with clothes in various stages of being made or repaired – all of them much grander than the clothes worn by the seamstress and the girl, who were now exchanging looks as if they thought this was very strange behaviour for a princess.

'I am Dinah, the palace seamstress, and this is Tilly, my apprentice,' the old lady told her, sounding a little guarded. 'Have you a dress or some other garment that needs repairing, Your Highness?'

'Well . . . do you have . . . I mean, do you think you could . . . find another bow for this bridesmaid's dress?' Ava asked, bunching up the material at the front of her skirt to show where the missing bow should be.

Tilly gave a little grin and pulled something out of her sewing box. 'What about this one?' she asked, holding up a gold silk bow identical to the others on Ava's dress.

'That's it! That's the missing bow!' Ava exclaimed. 'Where did you find it?'

'Dinah found it yesterday in the palace kitchens,' Tilly told her. 'She was there speaking to the palace cook, when she noticed one of the kitchen cats had something caught in its claw.'

Ava turned to Dinah excitedly. 'Was it a *tabby* cat?'

The old lady frowned as if she was trying her best to remember. 'I believe it might have been a tabby, Your Highness . . . yes . . .'

'Where is this cat now?' Ava asked, jumping to her feet. 'Is it still in the kitchen?'

'I expect so – Cook likes to keep them there because cats are so good at keeping the mice away.'

'We have to go and look for her!' Ava

exclaimed, taking an impatient step towards the door. 'She's not a kitchen cat, you see. She's my pet cat, Cindy, and I have to find her!'

'A *pet* cat!' Dinah looked surprised. 'Well I never!'

'I can take you to the kitchens if you like,' Tilly offered. She looked at Dinah. 'If you can spare me for a little while.'

Dinah nodded. 'Hurry back though. We've a lot of work to do before the ball tonight.'

'Don't worry. I'll just show Princess Ava the way and I'll come straight back,' Tilly promised.

Ava almost blurted out that she wasn't *really* a princess – because somehow she felt bad about lying to these two servants – but she stopped herself. After all, she was very close to finding Cindy now, and she didn't want to say or do anything that might ruin things.

6

Tilly led Ava along the corridor and through a doorway that led to a narrow flight of spiral stairs. 'This is the servants' staircase,' Tilly explained. 'It's the quickest way to the kitchens. You don't mind, do you, Your Highness?'

'Of course not,' Ava said.

The staircase went down a long way. After a while Ava became aware of cooking smells, and finally they reached the bottom, where Tilly stopped to push open a heavy oak door.

Now they were in a vast kitchen full of

servants. It was very like the one Ava had
seen when she'd visited a National Trust
stately home with her mother. Except
that there the servants had been waxwork
figures, whereas here they were real. At one
end of the room there was a massive stone
fireplace with a huge fire that was giving off
a terrific amount of heat. An enormous pig

was being roasted over the fire while a maid (who was dripping with sweat) poked at the logs underneath. Elsewhere in the kitchen other maids were standing at big stone work surfaces, chopping up vegetables, rolling out pastry and performing various other tasks with great speed. Two maids stood at a massive cooking range stirring the contents of several huge pans. The noise of all this activity, in addition to the shrill voices of the senior maids shouting orders at the junior ones, was deafening.

Tilly leaned closer to Ava and said, 'I'll ask Cook to come and speak with you.'

Ava watched Tilly dodge across the kitchen, skirting around the hard-working maids in order to approach an older, plumpish woman on the other side of the room, who was overseeing the plucking of

a pair of pheasants. The young maid who was doing it was obviously too slow for the cook's liking, because the cook kept prodding her and shouting that she would box her ears if she didn't speed up.

Ava thought Tilly was very brave to interrupt the impatient cook – but clearly the fact that she had come on an errand for a princess made all the difference. As soon as Tilly pointed to Ava, the cook quickly used her apron to wipe the sweat from her brow and came to greet Ava with a polite smile on her face.

She gave a little curtsy before saying, 'Tilly says you're looking for your cat, Your Highness.'

Ava nodded and the cook shook her head sadly. 'If only you'd come just a few hours earlier, Your Highness . . .'

'What do you mean?' Ava asked, starting to feel butterflies in her tummy again.

'Well, only this morning we had a visit from Cinderella's fairy godmother. She was collecting animals, you see. You know how she likes to turn mice into horses and lizards into footman and rats into coach drivers and the like? Well, we gave her all the mice from the mousetrap – she's given us a special one to use that catches them but doesn't actually kill them – and a rabbit that was too skinny to make stew out of, which we kept alive for her too. I mean, after all that, I felt we'd done our bit down here in the kitchens, I really did, but *then* she said she was looking for some cats and dogs as well. I said we couldn't help with the dogs but since we've got quite a few cats here she could have the first one she could catch. Well – that tabby

one went up to her the second she wafted some fish under its nose.'

'Oh no,' Ava murmured, thinking how much Cindy loved to eat fish. 'Where did the fairy godmother take her?'

'I'm afraid I couldn't say, Your Highness,' replied the cook politely. 'I expect she's taken her off to wherever it is that she concocts her spells. Now, if you'll excuse me, I must be getting back to my work.'

'I *have* to find Cindy before anything happens to her!' Ava exclaimed to Tilly as they left the kitchen together. 'You don't think the fairy godmother would actually *hurt* her, do you? After all, she's a *good* character . . . I mean, *person* . . . isn't she?' she added quickly.

'She's certainly a character-and-a-half and no mistake!' Tilly answered, grinning. 'Most people reckon she *means* well most of the time – but she's very temperamental and she tends to fly off the handle on a regular basis! She's obsessed with inventing new spells and nobody's ever quite sure what she's going to come up with next!'

Ava frowned. Somehow she had expected the characters in fairytale land to be a lot more straightforward – like they were in her fairytale book. 'Do you have any idea where she might be right now?' she asked Tilly anxiously.

'I don't know about right now,' Tilly answered. 'But tonight she'll definitely be at the ball.'

'The ball?' Ava queried.

'The special eve-of-the-wedding ball. Everybody is going to it. And the fairy godmother will definitely be there because

she has to help at the dress competition.'

'The *dress* competition?'

'Surely you've heard about it, Your Highness,' Tilly said. 'When Cinderella and Prince Charming got engaged they announced that there would be a special competition in honour of their marriage – a competition that absolutely anyone in the palace is allowed to enter – even the servants! Cinderella is going to award a prize to whoever makes the most original and beautiful dress – which they may wear tonight to the ball. Cinderella is to choose the winner and the prize will be to have a magic wish granted by the fairy godmother!'

'Wow!' Ava exclaimed. 'That sounds amazing!'

Tilly had a strange look on her face as she

blurted, 'It's a once-in-a-lifetime chance! At least, it *could* have been.'

'What do you mean?' Ava asked, puzzled.

Tilly sniffed and rubbed her nose. 'It's just that I've always wanted to have my own dress shop one day, but – as Dinah says – a poor servant like me could never afford it. So I thought . . . I thought with the help of a magic wish, maybe it *could* happen, so . . .'

'You decided to enter the competition?'

Tilly nodded. 'I've spent all my spare time for the last few months making a dress from the material that was left over after we'd made gowns for the queen and the princesses and the ladies-in-waiting and all the other members of the royal household. Just small scraps that would have been thrown away otherwise – but together they made a beautiful multicoloured dress fit for

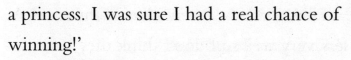

a princess. I was sure I had a real chance of winning!'

'So what happened?' Ava asked, guessing from Tilly's face that something must have.

'One day last week my dress was stolen from the sewing room. Dinah had gone to lie down because she wasn't feeling well, and I went to measure one of the ugly sisters for a new gown. When I got back the dress was gone.'

'That's terrible!' Ava exclaimed. 'But who could have taken it? And why?'

'I don't know.' There were tears in Tilly's eyes as she continued, 'But now there's no time to make another dress for the competition.'

Ava was looking thoughtful. 'Are the two ugly sisters entering this competition too?' she asked.

Tilly nodded. 'But neither of them can sew very well so I don't think they have much chance of winning!'

'You said you were measuring one of them when your dress went missing?' Ava reminded her.

'That's right – Ermentrude wanted a new gown.'

'Was Astrid there as well?'

'No. She was taking an afternoon nap.'

'Hmm . . .'

Tilly sighed as if she already knew what Ava was thinking. 'You're wondering if Astrid stole the dress while Ermentrude was keeping me distracted with her fitting, aren't you?'

'Well, they *do* seem like the most likely thieves,' Ava agreed.

'That's what *I* thought too. I mean, I know

they can't *wear* my dress, because neither
of them would fit into it. But at least by
taking it they've knocked me out of the
competition, which gives their own dresses
a better chance of winning. But when I
said that to Dinah she said I had to be very
cautious about accusing them, because they're
Cinderella's sisters, which means they're
practically royalty too. She said I'd need to
have proof first – and I haven't got any.'

'I see what she means,' Ava murmured,
thinking about how dangerous it could be
for a servant to get on the wrong side of the
ugly sisters.

'So even if Ermentrude and Astrid did
steal my dress, there's nothing I can do
about it,' Tilly said sadly. 'I guess I've just
got to accept that I'll *never* have my own
dress shop now.'

Ava thought about what *she* did when she wanted something really badly, but couldn't see any way of getting it. 'Have you talked to your mum and dad about it?' she asked.

'My parents died when I was very small,' Tilly told her.

'Oh.' Ava was shocked and didn't know what else to say. 'That's awful,' she finally mumbled.

Tilly nodded. 'But I was lucky because Dinah saw me begging outside the palace that winter and asked if I'd like to learn how to be a seamstress like her. I was very little then and the winter was so cold that year that I'd probably have died myself if it hadn't been for her. Even though I was too young to be much help to her to start with, she still shared her food with me and let me snuggle up in bed while she worked into

the night. She even made me
a doll to play with – a little
ragdoll with buttons for eyes
and soft woollen hair.'

'Dinah must be a very
kind person,' Ava said.

'She is,' Tilly agreed.
'She's taught me everything
she knows, plus she says I have a natural flair
for sewing. Now, because her eyesight isn't
so good and her hands are getting shaky, I'm
better at it than she is – and a lot faster. She
can't even thread a needle very easily any
more so I have to do that for her.'

'It must be an important job being the
palace seamstress,' Ava said.

'Yes it is, but we have to work very hard
and everyone bosses us around all the time,
wanting their clothes to be ready far more

quickly than we can do them. That's why I'd really love to get away from here one day . . .' She sighed. 'Never mind. Maybe my dress wouldn't have won the competition in any case. But I'd really *love* to be going to that ball!'

Ava frowned, desperately wanting to help. 'Couldn't you *borrow* a dress to wear?' she suggested, an idea forming in her head. 'One that's just as beautiful as the missing dress . . .'

'Where would I possibly find such a thing?' Tilly asked in a disbelieving voice.

Ava grinned as she replied, 'Leave it to me – I know of a very good shop near here where I'm allowed to borrow any dress that I like!'

7

After Tilly had sewn the gold bow back on
Ava's dress, Ava asked her new friend to
show her the way back to the music room.

When they got there, the dancing
princesses had left (thankfully) and the music
box was still sitting on the table.

'Thanks, Tilly. I'll come and find you
later when I've got the dress, and we can go
to the ball together,' Ava promised, eager to
be alone so that she could make her escape.
She hoped her dad hadn't been too worried
about her while she was gone. Still, she
reassured herself quickly, it wasn't as if he

hadn't known where she was – sort of.

Carefully she opened the lid of the music box and stared as hard as she could at her reflection in the little mirror inside. To her huge relief the mirror instantly began to glow. Ava kept looking into it with as much concentration as she could, until the mirror became too bright to look any longer. Then she closed her eyes.

Just as before, the brightness soon passed and after a few seconds Ava nervously opened her eyes again.

'*Yes!*' she exclaimed jubilantly as she looked around and saw that she was surrounded by wedding dresses, safely back in the upstairs room of Marietta's shop.

Incredibly, no time at all seemed to have passed since she'd left – because the first thing she heard was her father's footsteps on

the spiral stairs and his angry voice calling out, 'Ava! Are you up there?'

Desperately Ava looked around for somewhere to hide. It wasn't that she was truly scared of her father – but she couldn't allow him to stop her returning to fairytale land before she had rescued Cindy and helped Tilly.

She ended up crawling under the nearest wedding dress. Its full skirt, which fell to the floor, hid her completely like a tent. She only just got there in time as her dad arrived at the top of the stairs and called her name again. Then she heard him walk slowly around the room.

'Where is she, Marietta?' he asked crossly as Marietta arrived at the top of the stairs too.

'I told you – she's still travelling.'

'So which mirror did she go through?'
Dad demanded.

'I'm not telling you,' Marietta answered
firmly. 'You'll only go there and spoil it for her. You'll just have to wait until she gets back – it can't be long now.'

'She's been gone for over two hours!' Dad growled. 'What if something's happened to her?'

110

Ava listened to this with interest. If two hours had passed since she had last been in Marietta's shop, then time couldn't have stood still after all.

'I expect she's found lots of exciting things to do there,' Marietta said. 'You may as well go home again and I'll ring you when she returns.'

'I've already *been* home,' her dad said angrily. 'And now I'm back and she's *still* not here! It's just not on, Marietta! She has no experience of this sort of thing!'

'And whose fault is that?' Marietta said quietly.

'Don't start that again!' Dad retorted. 'I've done the right thing, keeping her away from all this for as long as I could.'

'Except that you've kept her away from yourself in the process!'

'I wanted her to lead a normal life with her mother,' Dad said sharply. 'And she has done – until *now*, that is.'

'She *can't* lead a normal life, Otto,' Marietta said passionately, 'and the sooner you realize that the better. The travelling gift is in her blood! Anyway, I don't see *you* turning your back on it, to pursue a *normal* life, as you call it!'

As the two adults started to walk back downstairs, Ava crawled out from her hiding place. She was intrigued by what she had just heard, and her mind was spinning with questions, but now she had to concentrate on picking out a dress for Tilly to wear for the competition. She also had to choose another dress for herself – a ball gown to wear this evening.

As she got to her feet, all she was thinking

about was how soon her dad was going to leave so that she could ask Marietta to help her.

'AVA!'

She jumped with fright, whirling round to see her father, who had crept back up to the top of the staircase. He must have heard the rustling as she'd come out of hiding.

'Dad,' she said in a shaky voice.

'Ava – where have you been? I've been worried sick!' he exclaimed angrily.

'Sorry,' she mumbled hoarsely. And suddenly his anger on top of everything else was too much – and she burst into tears.

Back downstairs as Marietta gave her a hug and started to say something sympathetic, Dad said crossly, 'You keep out of this, Marietta – you've done enough already!'

He was clearly much more angry with Marietta than he was with Ava, who was still sobbing loudly. He even made an awkward attempt to comfort Ava himself, mumbling, 'There, there – no need for that,' as he pulled out a grubby-looking hanky to mop up her tears.

'Shall I make us all a cup of tea?' Marietta suggested soothingly.

But Dad just glared at her and said that he was taking Ava home immediately.

'But maybe I can help you explain things, Otto,' Marietta said, frowning.

'I am perfectly capable of explaining things myself, thank you, Marietta,' he snapped. 'Come on, Ava. It's time to get changed back into your own clothes.'

Ava had no choice but to do as he said. Thankfully, by the time she emerged in her ordinary clothes from Marietta's fairytale changing room, she was feeling a lot more together and a lot more determined. 'Does the time pass just as quickly on the other side of the mirrors as it does here?' she asked Marietta as she pushed back the sparkly curtain to hand her the green and gold bridesmaid's dress, followed by the tiara and the emerald shoes.

As Marietta replied that it did, Dad asked suspiciously, 'Why do you want to know that?'

'Oh, I just wondered,' Ava replied guardedly, but in fact she was trying to calculate how long she had before the ball – and the dress competition – took place that night.

'When we get home I'll explain everything,' her father told her as they left the shop together. 'But I don't want you using the mirrors again. At least not until I think you're ready – do you understand?'

When she didn't answer, he repeated more forcefully, 'Do you understand, Ava?'

'Of course,' she murmured sullenly.

Of course she understood that he didn't *want* her to use them – but that wasn't the same as promising not to, was it?

8

It didn't take them long to get back to the house, and Dad immediately asked Ava to sit down while he made them both a cup of tea.

'I don't like tea,' she snapped, but he ignored her and went into his study, coming back with a small blue tin with a teddy bear on the front.

'This is special tea,' he told her. 'I've had it since I was your age. I'm not sure how it's made exactly, but when I was a boy I thought it was the most delicious drink imaginable. You can taste it for yourself in a minute and see what *you* think.'

'I told you, I don't want any tea,' Ava
said impatiently, sure that her dad was just
stalling for time. 'I want you to explain
everything.'

Dad sighed. 'The fact is – this tea will *help*
me explain, because it reminds me of how
I felt when I was *your* age.' He spoke very
carefully as he continued. 'When *I* was a
child I went travelling with my parents from
an early age, but it wasn't until my ninth
birthday that they let me go on my first trip
through a mirror alone.' He smiled as he
remembered. 'They arranged for me to go
and see Father Christmas. The *real* Father
Christmas!'

Ava gaped at him, hardly able to believe
he was serious.

'It was the middle of the summer, so he

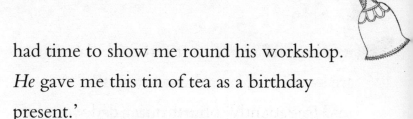

had time to show me round his workshop. *He* gave me this tin of tea as a birthday present.'

Ava just gazed at him incredulously.

'You might think that was a funny sort of birthday present to give a little boy, right?' Dad continued.

Speechless, she nodded, because it was true that she had always imagined Father Christmas's workshop to be full of shiny new train sets and beautiful dolls, rather than tins of tea.

'Well, it isn't just ordinary tea,' her father explained. '*He* called it *fizzy* tea – but in fact it does a lot more than fizz. When you drink

119 🌸🌸🌸

it, it can tell what your favourite flavours
are – and it creates them for you!'

'*Magic* tea!' Ava burst out.

'There must certainly be some magic
in the ingredients, yes,' her dad agreed.
'Anyway, I drank most of it as a boy, but I
put the last few spoonfuls away – because I
couldn't bear the thought of it being gone
completely. I've saved what was left for all
these years, waiting for an occasion that was
special enough to bring it out again.'

As he took the tin into the kitchen Ava
followed him, her mind racing. 'But you still
haven't told me about the mirrors, Dad. Are
we a family of witches or something? Is that
how we can travel through them?'

Her dad laughed. 'No, Ava. We aren't
witches. It's just that *we* can use the magic
mirrors whereas most people can't.' He

paused, looking more solemn. 'I know you must be feeling very confused right now, Ava. I guess the first thing you need to know is that you come from a long line of people who have an exceptional gift – the gift of being able to travel through magic portals. It's an ability that seems to be inherited from one generation to the next – a magic gene that gets passed on, if you like. It sounds crazy, I know. Don't worry – I'm going to answer all your questions in a minute. But first I want you to taste this tea.'

Ava watched her father use the end of a teaspoon to prise the lid off the tin. Then he took out a spoonful of tea and showed it to her. It looked exactly like ordinary tea and it didn't smell of anything at all. He placed a spoonful into each mug before filling them with cold water from the tap.

121

'Shouldn't you use boiling water from the kettle?' Ava asked in surprise.

'Not for this tea. The leaves will heat up the water to just the right temperature for drinking.' He handed her a mug. 'Now watch and wait.'

First Ava heard the liquid fizzing – then she saw it. Inside the mug some sort of special magic reaction seemed to be taking place. As Ava watched, the liquid was changing from clear to brown to green to pink to yellow to blue to red to orange and on and on through every colour Ava could imagine.

'It won't stop changing colour even when you're drinking it,' her dad told her. 'Don't worry – it's perfectly safe.'

Ava took a small, cautious sip. The drink tasted like warm toffee in her mouth.

Her second – longer – sip tasted of lemon bonbons. 'That's amazing!' Ava exclaimed. 'Whenever I'm choosing sweets I can never decide between lemon bonbons or toffee ones. And Mum always gets impatient and moans that they're both equally bad for my teeth!'

Dad's eyes were twinkling – something she didn't often see. 'Take another sip,' he urged her.

She did, and instantly giggled. 'Toothpaste flavour,' she burst out. 'But very *nice* toothpaste!'

'Father Christmas pops in something to help clean your teeth after anything that's very sweet,' Dad said. 'Very conscientious of him, wouldn't you say?'

'Very,' Ava agreed, still giggling. 'Can I drink the whole lot?'

'Of course,' Dad said, taking a gulp of his own drink. 'Liquorice Allsorts!' he exclaimed. 'Delicious!'

Ava smiled, but she still had a lot of questions. 'Why did you never tell me about Marietta and her shop before, Dad?' she asked. 'Marietta wanted you to, didn't she?'

Her father carefully put down his mug. 'Marietta, as you probably already know, can also travel through the mirrors, though her main job is to stay and look after the shop.' He paused. '*She* thinks our ability to travel through the portals is so much a part of us that it's not natural to try and pretend it isn't there. And *she* thinks that children with the gift should grow up knowing about it and using it from the beginning.' He paused again. 'But *I* think differently. *I* think it is too much for a child to understand – especially if one of its parents is a *non*-gifted human, like your mother. I believe it is better to wait until a child has reached adulthood before introducing them to the portals. Then at least they are old enough to assess for themselves all the risks involved.'

'*What* risks?' Ava asked, frowning.

'The gift of travelling is not always an easy gift to have, Ava. It can be exciting, yes, and there are plenty of places I'd love to take you in a few years' time. But the reason I don't want you travelling until you're older is that sometimes things can go wrong on the other side of the mirrors. Not all the places there are good ones, and in some you might experience things that you wish you hadn't.'

'What sorts of things?' she asked curiously.

Her father looked at her steadily, as if he was weighing up whether or not to tell her more. Finally he said slowly, 'Well . . . a few weeks ago, when I visited Victorian Britain, I saw a chimney sweep younger than you die after getting stuck up a chimney.'

'That's terrible!' she gasped.

'It was very frightening – and I wish I hadn't been there. It's one thing reading about that sort of thing in a book – but quite another actually seeing it for yourself.'

He swallowed, and Ava was surprised to see tears in his eyes.

Now she remembered that he was writing a book on Victorian children. 'Is *that* how you do your research for your books?' she asked. 'By using the mirrors and actually *going* back in time?'

He nodded. 'For a long time now I have been using my gift to document what life was like in days gone by. Marietta also has some historical men's outfits in her shop. I use them quite a lot.'

'So when we don't hear from you for ages and Mum says you're travelling with your work – is *that* what you're doing?'

He nodded again. 'Sometimes I live in other time periods for weeks or months on end. It's the only way to get a real feel for that time in history.'

'Does Mum know the truth?' Even as she asked it Ava was sure that her mum didn't.

'No. She isn't a traveller so she'd never understand. That was another reason I didn't want *you* to know yet, Ava – because I didn't like the idea of asking you to keep such a big secret from your mother.'

'Maybe Mum would understand, if *I* explained it to her,' Ava said.

'Or maybe she'd get such a fright that she'd never let me see you again,' Dad replied grimly.

'She wouldn't do that,' Ava said. 'She's always saying that she *wants* me to spend more time with you.'

'You *can't* tell her, Ava,' Dad said firmly. 'Not if you want her to keep letting you come and stay with me. Trust me on this, OK?'

'OK.' Ava listened quietly as Dad went on to talk about how everyone in his family was born with the special gift of being able to travel to other times in history, and even to fantasy worlds that various people had dreamed up at one time or another and which existed in the space between what was real and what was not.

He told how there were many places in *this* world where certain magic energies all clustered together to form magic portals that allowed entry to *other* worlds. And Marietta's shop was one of those places.

'The plot of land where the shop stands has been in our family for generations,' he added, 'though it was an ordinary house rather than a shop when my parents lived there – and my grandparents and great-grandparents before them.'

Ava had never heard her father mention his family before. All she knew was what her mother had told her – that Dad's parents had died a long time ago. Ava had always felt a bit strange asking questions about them, but now seemed like the right moment.

'Dad, how did your parents die?' she asked gently.

He frowned. 'Twelve years ago – not long before I met your mother – my parents went on a trip through one of the portals. They never returned.'

'That's terrible!' Ava exclaimed. 'What happened to them?'

'I don't know. Presumably, they are still living happily ever after.'

Ava was puzzled. 'I don't understand. I thought you said they died?'

'They might as well have done,' her

father said bluntly. 'They left a note saying that they had decided to go and live for good in one particular fantasy land that they'd found. Since such a thing is totally against the laws of our people – and a search party would most certainly have been sent after them to bring them back – they destroyed the portal they had travelled through to make sure no one could follow them. Destroying a portal is very difficult and very dangerous – but it can be done if you know how.'

'It must have been a really wonderful place if they wanted to stay there forever,' Ava said wide-eyed, because however exciting her trip to Cinderella-land had been, she couldn't imagine never wanting to come home again.

'It doesn't matter *how* wonderful it was –

they had no right to do that to me and my
sister,' Dad said, scowling.

'*Sister?*' This was news to Ava.

Dad looked at her. 'That's right – a
younger sister who was only sixteen when
my parents left.'

'A *sister!*' Ava still couldn't believe it.

'We don't always get on very well,' Dad
added drily.

'Where does she live? When can I meet
her?' Ava asked breathlessly.

Dad was giving her a very sober look
now, as if she was being incredibly stupid.

And that's when it dawned on her. 'You
don't mean . . . you can't mean . . . ? Dad, is
Marietta your sister?'

'Marietta and I both grew up in that little corner house,' Dad explained. 'It was Marietta's idea to turn it into a shop after our parents left.'

Ava stared at him in amazement. 'You mean, I had an aunt all this time and I didn't even *know*!' she blurted out.

Her father looked apologetic. 'I didn't want you to find out about the magic portals, and I knew that if I let you meet Marietta she'd see to it that you did. She was meant to be going away for the whole of this summer – the shop was to be closed for

a while – but at the last minute she changed
her plans. Of course as soon as she heard you
were coming she got all excited. I suppose I
should have expected that she'd make herself
known to you somehow.' He scowled. 'She
won't admit it, but I'm sure she deliberately
used Cindy to lure you into the shop.'

'What do you mean?' Ava was confused.

'Marietta happened to phone me on the
day Cindy went missing so I mentioned to
her that we were searching for your cat. She
was very interested – asking me exactly what
Cindy looked like – and I told her about
the white patch on her front paw and that
little nick she's got on her right ear. I asked
Marietta to keep an eye out for her and to
give me a ring if she saw her. Anyway, I
think Marietta did more than just keep an
eye out. I think she went and hunted high

and low for Cindy until she found her. But instead of letting me know, she took her back to the shop and put that notice on the door to tempt *you* inside.'

Ava frowned. 'But how could she guess I'd walk past her shop and actually *see* the notice? I mean, *you* might have walked by and seen it first!'

'Oh, she knows I don't go near her shop when you're staying with me. And she also knows your instincts would soon take you in that direction. The portals are a bit like magnets to people who can travel through them. We sort of get drawn towards them without even being aware of it. You've been sensitive to the magic in the portals ever since you were tiny, Ava – that's why I've always known that the travelling gift has been passed on to you. I don't think you realize the number of times you've started to walk towards Marietta's shop when you've visited me before – and I've always steered you off along another route.'

'Really?' Ava was surprised – and a little bit thrilled at the thought of being drawn towards the magic portals like that. Then she thought about her cat and frowned again. 'But it's not fair of Marietta to use Cindy in that way.'

'I know,' Dad said.

'And *then* she let her disappear through a magic mirror!' Ava exclaimed indignantly.

Her dad nodded grimly. 'That was very irresponsible. I'm sure she didn't mean that to happen.'

Ava sat very still as she let everything sink in.

'Ava, I know you think I haven't been

around for you very much up till now,' her
dad said, sounding a little uncomfortable.
'But my priority has always been for you
to have what I didn't have – a normal
childhood.'

Ava thought about all the times she had
worried that it was *her* fault that her dad
didn't want to see her more often.

'You could have come to visit me more,'
she said in a small voice. 'Or taken me away
for a holiday somewhere. Then I wouldn't
have had to come anywhere near Marietta's
shop.'

'I'm sorry, Ava,' Dad said sombrely. 'I
guess I was just afraid that the more time
you spent with me the more chance there
was that you'd find out my secret. It's very
difficult to keep a thing like this from people
you're close to.'

'So you thought it was safer if we *weren't* close?' Ava said.

Dad met her gaze as he replied, 'Yes, I suppose I did.'

'So how come you let me stay with you for such a long time *this* summer?' Ava asked quietly.

Dad sighed. 'If I'm honest, I was worried about it at first, but since Marietta was meant to be going away I thought it would be all right, so long as I was careful about what you saw while you were here. I didn't mean to leave those books on magic lying about, for one thing. By the time Marietta told me she had changed her plans, it was too late to stop you coming.'

Ava had a sudden thought. 'Does *Mum* know about Marietta?'

Dad shook his head. 'It was easier not to

introduce them. Marietta thought I was a fool to marry your mum. She said the two of us could never be happy because of all the secret-keeping. The worst thing is that she was right.'

'But *why* couldn't you tell Mum?' Ava asked. 'She *might* have understood.'

'Would *you* have understood a thing like that? Would you have even believed it was possible before you experienced it for yourself?'

'I suppose if I actually *saw* a person disappearing through a mirror in front of me . . .' Ava murmured.

'You'd assume it was a magician's trick,' Dad said. 'Think about it, Ava. If a bright light forced you to close your eyes and then, when you opened them again, the person who'd been in front of you was gone, what would you think had happened? Would you think they had been transported through a magic mirror or would you assume a trick had been played on you?'

Ava was beginning to see his point. 'A trick,' she admitted.

'Exactly – and you wouldn't rest until you found out how it had been done. Only you never *would* find out . . .'

Both Ava and her dad were silent for a few moments, thinking about Ava's mother. Then Ava said, 'But now that *I*'ve found out, Dad – and now that I've travelled through a portal myself – I *have* to go back to Cinderella-land.'

'That's where you were?'

'Yes. And I *have* to go back there to find Cindy.'

Her dad looked solemn. 'I don't think

that's a good idea. Fairytale land isn't as safe as you think, Ava. There are plenty of baddies in fairytales – and they are usually very bad indeed. Think of the wicked witch in the story of Hansel and Gretel – or the evil queen who poisoned Snow White!'

'But the two ugly sisters are the baddies in Cinderella-land.' Ava told him. 'And although they did seem really horrible when I met them, I'm sure it will be easy enough to keep out of their way.'

Her father looked at her sharply. 'You've met the ugly sisters already?'

Ava nodded. 'I think they must be staying in the palace for Cinderella's wedding.'

141

She frowned because there was something that was puzzling her about Astrid and Ermentrude. 'Dad, why does everyone call them the *ugly* sisters? I mean, they're not all *that* ugly.'

'The description isn't to do with their appearance,' her father explained. 'They are called that because they have very little beauty or goodness *inside* them. And they are *extremely* ugly on the inside, believe me, judging by some of their past actions.'

'Like when they shut Cinderella in the cellar, you mean?' Ava said.

'That . . . and . . . well . . . it's never been proven, but apparently many people in fairytale land don't believe that the death of Cinderella's father was an accident.'

'What? You mean they think the ugly sisters *killed* him?' Ava asked, wide-eyed. In her fairytale book there had been no details given of exactly *how* Cinderella's father had died, she remembered.

'So I'm told. I haven't been to fairytale land myself for a long time, but Marietta heard that he fell down the cellar steps and broke his neck one day while the ugly sisters just happened to be alone in the house with him. They claimed to have nothing to do with it of course, and Cinderella believed them because Cinderella *always* believes the best about people.' He shook his head a little impatiently. 'I know she can't help the nature she's been given, but sometimes I think Cinderella has too *much* goodness inside her. I mean, why on earth would she invite her stepsisters to the wedding?'

'I guess she must be *very* forgiving,' Ava said.

'*Too* forgiving, if you ask me,' her dad grunted. 'Like I said before, none of the rumours have ever been proven – but if *anyone* should go back to fairytale land to fetch Cindy, it should be Marietta or myself, not you.'

'No, Dad. *I* have to be the one to go,' Ava insisted. 'It's not just to fetch Cindy. There's a girl there whom I promised to help too! Don't worry – I'll be really careful to stay away from the ugly sisters. *They're* scared of *me* now, in any case, because they think I'm a ghost!'

'A ghost?' Ava's dad was clearly about to ask more, when the phone started ringing.

He quickly went to answer it. 'Hello, Marietta . . . Yes, I've told her . . .' There was a long pause while he listened.

'*What?* . . . Are you sure? . . . OK, OK, just

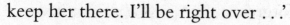

keep her there. I'll be right over ...'

'What's wrong?' Ava asked when he came off the phone.

'Marietta has a visitor in her shop,' he said, frowning.

'What visitor?' Ava asked curiously.

'A nanny whom I met on my last visit to Victorian London. She's a travelling person like us and she must have been watching the last time I came back through the portal because she followed me through it. And now that she's discovered it, the daft woman seems to think she can come and go as she pleases.'

'But why shouldn't she – if *she* has the gift too?' Ava asked, puzzled.

'Because for *her*, this is the future. And it is forbidden for any of us to visit the future.'

'Really? Why?'

'It's complicated. All you have to know
for now is that it's against our laws, Ava.
Even when we travel *back* in time, we have
to be careful not to give too much away
about where we come from. If this nanny
gets discovered here, Marietta's shop might
be closed down.'

'That sounds serious.'

'It is – which is why I have to go there at
once.'

'Can I come too?' Ava asked, excited at
the prospect of getting to meet a real nanny
from Victorian times.

But her father shook his head. 'The less
contact the nanny has with people here, the
better.'

'You can't just leave me in the house on
my own,' Ava pointed out, a little sulkily.

'Fine. You can come with me to the

shop, but you'll have to wait for me in the front room while Marietta and I sort this out.'

Marietta gave Ava an excited hug when she greeted her at the door, clearly delighted that she could now be open about the fact that Ava was her niece. Ava found it difficult to suddenly think of Marietta as her aunt – but she guessed maybe that would come in time. After all, *she* had only just learned about Marietta, whereas Marietta had known about *her* ever since she'd been born.

'Wait here, Ava,' Dad said, pointing to a small, uncomfortable-looking chair in the dreary front section of the shop. 'Hopefully this won't take *too* long.' He turned to Marietta and asked, 'Where is she?'

'Follow me.'

147

After they had both disappeared through the beaded curtain, Ava got up and went to peer through it herself. They weren't in the fairytale room on the other side, so Ava could only assume Marietta had taken Dad to a room even further back inside the shop.

Ava quickly pushed through the curtain and went to look for a dress for Tilly. It would have been better if she could have asked Marietta's permission before borrowing another dress, but she couldn't do that without alerting Dad. Besides, she had a feeling Marietta would approve of what she was doing in any case.

After several minutes of trying to make up her mind, Ava pulled out the four dresses that looked like they would fit Tilly the best. One was yellow with cream bows, one was pale blue with a lacy bodice, one was

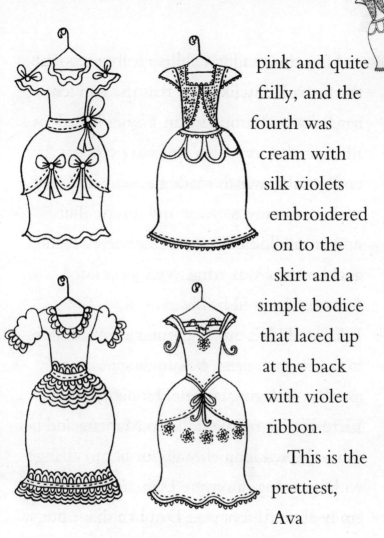

pink and quite frilly, and the fourth was cream with silk violets embroidered on to the skirt and a simple bodice that laced up at the back with violet ribbon.

This is the prettiest, Ava thought, slipping the cream and violet one from its hanger.

She then had to choose a dress for herself,

and her eye caught a child's ball gown that was remarkably like one that she had for her Princess Barbie doll at home. It had a long red skirt with a stiff red petticoat underneath, which made the skirt stick out without having to wear any hoops. The simple red bodice had a pretty heart-shaped neckline and was attractively decorated with shimmering gold beads.

Excited, Ava quickly found a pair of shoes to match each dress, before disappearing into the changing cubicle. Hopefully the Victorian nanny would keep Marietta and her dad occupied long enough for her to change without being discovered. She felt slightly guilty about disobeying Dad like this – but only slightly. He didn't always know what was best for her, she decided. It was *her* job to rescue Cindy and help Tilly – and besides

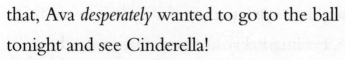

that, Ava *desperately* wanted to go to the ball tonight and see Cinderella!

Once she was ready – and she was delighted with how glamorous she looked in her new dress – she hurried up the spiral staircase and found to her relief that the music box was exactly where she had left it. Holding on tightly to Tilly's shoes, and with the cream and violet dress draped carefully over her arm, Ava opened the lid of the box.

Would the ball gown she was now wearing transport her through the mirror in the music box, just as the bridesmaid's dress had done? It came from Marietta's fairytale collection too, so surely it should. But would it matter that she was carrying with her an extra fairytale dress? Unfortunately Ava just didn't yet know all the rules when it came to travelling through the portals – and there

151

was nobody she could ask.

Feeling nervous, she looked into the mirror, holding her breath as she waited for the magic reaction to start up. There was nothing left to do now but take a chance . . . and keep her fingers crossed that nothing would go wrong.

As soon as Ava arrived back in the palace music room she heaved a huge sigh of relief. Her new red ball gown had made the magic happen just as well as the bridesmaid's dress had done – and Tilly's dress and shoes had also passed through the portal unharmed. But she decided that it was best to play it safe from now on, by keeping the music box in her possession. That way she knew she could return home through the portal at any time she chose.

The clock on the wall told her that it was nearly half past six already, which meant that if she was to get Tilly's outfit to her in time for the competition she would have to hurry.

'Look who it is!' a snide voice exclaimed as she stepped out of the music room into the corridor.

Ava froze as she found herself face to face with Astrid and Ermentrude.

Unfortunately they no longer looked frightened of her.

'She doesn't look much like a ghost now, does she, Ermentude?' the blonde-haired sister sneered.

'No,' the dark one snapped. 'It was obviously some sort of trick.' She glared menacingly at Ava. 'And now we're going to make you tell us how you did it!'

Astrid suddenly spotted the music box, half concealed by Tilly's dress. 'What's that?' she snarled, reaching out and grabbing the box before Ava could stop her. 'Look, Ermentrude! She's clearly a thief!'

'I was only borrowing it!' Ava protested. 'Please give it back!'

Ermentrude laughed nastily. 'Let *me* see the box, Astrid. Is it valuable?'

'I don't know, but *I'm* keeping it! It will look perfect on my dressing table!' Astrid grinned slyly at Ava. 'If anyone notices it's missing we'll tell them *you* stole it! After all, *you'll* be too scared to tell them anything by the time *we've* finished with you!'

Ava started to feel frightened, but fortunately at that moment Ermentrude made a grab for the box herself, snarling, '*You're* not keeping it, Astrid. I'm the older

sister so *I* should have it!'

Ava seized her chance to escape while they were still bickering. She lifted up the long skirt of her gown and rushed as fast as she could away from them.

'After her!' Astrid yelled at once – but the ugly sisters weren't very quick on their feet and Ava soon managed to outrun them.

She headed for the sewing room, trying not to let the feelings of panic overwhelm her. The ugly sisters had the music box! And for as long as they had it she wouldn't be able to return home again! She *had* to think of a way of getting it back from them – but what if she couldn't? Did that mean she would be stuck in fairytale land forever?

'Princess Ava!' Tilly exclaimed in surprise, starting to curtsy as she opened the sewing-room door to Ava. 'Are you all right? You look as though you've just had an awful shock.'

Ava's stomach was churning as she thought about the music box, but she couldn't explain that to Tilly. 'I'm fine,' she said, doing her best to sound normal. 'I found you another dress to wear. Look.'

Tilly looked uncertain as Ava held up the cream and violet ball gown to show her. 'It's lovely, Your Highness, but I don't know. I've been thinking about it. Wouldn't it be cheating to enter a dress into the competition that isn't my own creation?'

Ava supposed that it probably *was* cheating. But after her most recent encounter with the ugly sisters – who were almost certainly the ones who had stolen Tilly's original dress – she felt determined

that they shouldn't get to ruin *everything*.

'Oh, but it's only fair that you get to go to the ball after all your hard work,' she insisted.

Tilly was slowly inspecting the gown. 'I *would* really love to go to the ball,' she said. 'And I suppose it can't do any harm to wear this dress tonight if it fits me, since I'm sure it won't actually win.' She flushed as she added quickly, 'It's really pretty – but I'm sure the winning dress has got to be a bit *different* from normal dresses – more *original*, if you see what I mean. Don't you think so, Dinah?'

The elderly seamstress nodded, looking thoughtful as she said, 'Yes, Tilly, I do. That dress is very pretty – but I've seen many others just like it.'

Tilly agreed to try on the dress, and while

157 ❀❀❀

Dinah was helping her to change, Ava
suddenly remembered something important.
'Tilly, do you think Astrid and Ermentrude
will *definitely* be at the ball tonight?' she asked.

'Oh yes. Like I said before, they are both
entering the dress competition.'

'Good,' Ava murmured under her breath.
For Ava had remembered what her dad
had said about people with the travelling
gift being *drawn* towards the magic portals.
If that was true, then all she had to do was
follow her *instinct* and she would be *taken*
to wherever the ugly sisters had hidden the
music box. And as long as they remained
out of the way at the ball, Ava would have
the chance she needed to escape home with
Cindy – presuming she had found her by
that time of course.

She would just have to make sure the ugly

sisters didn't actually see her tonight, that
was all.

'You look lovely!' Ava exclaimed when
Tilly was ready.

'It's certainly an excellent fit,' Dinah said.

Making a big effort to smile bravely, Tilly
said, 'Thank you so much, Princess Ava. At
least now I can go to the ball.'

'That's all right.' Ava replied, smiling
back. 'But it must be due to start very soon,
isn't it? Hadn't we better get going?'

'The ball starts at seven o'clock, but the
competition isn't until eight,' Tilly said.
'I'll come along then because I need to
help Dinah finish off some needlework
first.'

'OK, but I think I'd better go now if I'm
to find the fairy godmother.'

'Just be aware of the fact that she might

have used your cat in a spell already,' Dinah
said warningly.

'Dinah!' Tilly exclaimed.

'I just want Princess Ava to be prepared,
that's all,' Dinah said defensively. 'It's better
to be prepared than to get a nasty shock. I've
had a good few nasty shocks in my life, so I
know what I'm talking about.'

'It's OK, Dinah. I *am* prepared,' Ava
reassured her.

But as she headed on her own to the
palace ballroom, taking care to follow Tilly's
directions precisely so as not to get lost, she
started to feel as if she wasn't prepared in
the slightest. After all, it wasn't every day
you had to rescue your cat from Cinderella's
fairy godmother, was it? I mean, how could
anyone be truly prepared for *that*?

10

The ball had already begun by the time
Ava got there. Lively music could be
heard coming from the ballroom, where
an important-looking manservant in a
white curly wig and gold-coloured jacket
and breeches was standing at the door
announcing all the guests. Nervously Ava
joined the small queue waiting to enter the
room, and she was pleased to see the friendly
young princess she had spoken to earlier,
who waved to her.

All the young princesses except Ava
seemed to be accompanied by their parents,

and Ava was given a strange look by
the manservant as she stood alone in the
doorway.

'Your name, Your Highness?' he enquired.

'P-P-Princess Ava,' Ava stammered,
cringing and going bright red as she said it.

But the manservant didn't bat an eyelid
as he effortlessly announced at the top of his
voice, 'HER ROYAL HIGHNESS THE
PRINCESS AVA!'

A few guests turned to look at her,
but most were too busy with their own
conversations to wonder why a child
princess had come to the ball alone.

Doing her best to rein in her nerves, Ava
walked into the ballroom holding her chin
up high as if she was balancing books on top
of her head – which was something she had
once heard all princesses were taught to do.

The ballroom, the walls of which were
made up entirely of mirrors, was beautifully
decorated, with glitter balls hanging from
the ceiling in between massive crystal
chandeliers. Free-standing candleholders
stood around the periphery bearing
enormous shimmering candles. The music
Ava had heard was coming from a string
quartet at one end of the room, and a few

163

guests were already dancing, the richly dressed women creating a colourful display in their beautiful gowns and sparkling jewellery as they waltzed with their handsome partners.

Around the edges of the dance floor, other guests were seated on ornate chairs, sipping glasses of champagne or fruit punch, while neatly dressed servants served delicious-looking finger food from silver trays. At the end furthest from the musicians four throne-like chairs had been placed, and Ava guessed that was where the King and Queen, and Cinderella and Prince Charming would sit when they arrived.

She started to scan the room for the fairy godmother, but since she didn't know what she looked like, it wasn't easy. How old was she, for one thing? And would she have visible wings like a regular fairy, or would they be hidden under her clothes? Might she be flying about the room waving her wand, or would she be trying to blend in with the other guests?

Ava decided to go and ask the princess she had spotted earlier for help.

The young princess was sitting on a seat beside her mother, looking at the diamond watch on her wrist and frowning.

'Hello.' Ava greeted her shyly. 'Isn't it a wonderful ball?'

The young princess looked up and gave her a friendly smile before saying in a hushed voice, 'It's quite pretty, I agree – though as it's my tenth ball this summer I must say I'm getting a little tired of them.' She sighed. 'Mama says it's something all princesses have to endure – the endless parties and balls. I

165

expect *you* feel a bit fed up with the whole thing too, don't you? What kingdom do you come from, by the way?'

Ava thought very fast. Avoiding the last part of the question, she gushed, 'Well, the thing is, I'm especially excited about *this* ball because I really want to meet Cinderella's fairy godmother. I'm not sure where she is though. Do *you* know?'

'Oh, I believe she's helping out with the dress competition. Cinderella was worried some of the entrants might cheat by wearing dresses they'd actually got someone *else* to make for them – so each entry is to be checked over by the fairy godmother first. Apparently she's got a magic spell which can tell her whether or not each dress was truly made by the person wearing it.'

'Oh no!' Ava blurted.

'What's wrong?' the princess asked in surprise.

'Nothing!' Ava replied quickly. 'I just really want to speak to her, that's all, and . . . and it sounds like she might be too busy.'

'Oh, look – there she is!' the princess exclaimed suddenly, pointing across the room at a plump, middle-aged lady who was holding a lace hanky over her nose as she ordered a maid to remove a large vase of pink flowers from a nearby table – complaining that the ghastly things were making her sneeze. She had curly white-blonde hair with

167

glittery bits in it and she was wearing a large purple and red ball gown with a huge skirt. As she turned slightly, Ava saw that her shimmering gold-coloured wrap was covering something bulky attached to her back, which Ava guessed must be her wings.

Ava thanked the princess and slowly approached the fairy godmother, desperately trying to think of a tactful way to ask her about Cindy.

'Excuse me, Fairy Godmother,' she said timidly.

Immediately the fairy godmother whirled round and peered at her suspiciously through her round gold-rimmed spectacles. 'Don't tell me you're *another* of my godchildren?' she exclaimed. 'They seem to be cropping up everywhere I go these days! Just because I helped Cinderella to marry a

prince, doesn't mean I intend to do the same
for the rest of you, you know! Now, which
one are you and what do *you* want?'

'I'm Ava,' Ava told her nervously. 'And
I'm actually *not* one of your godchildren.'

'You're *not*? Then why did you just call
me godmother?'

Ava flushed. 'Because . . . because that's
what Cinderella calls you and I don't know
your real name.'

The fairy godmother looked slightly
friendlier as she said, 'So you're a friend of
Cinderella's, are you? Good. At least you're
on *her* side and not the prince's.'

'Her side?'

'For the ceremony of course. His family
is far larger than hers and he has many more
guests at the wedding than she does. I'm
afraid it's going to look very uneven inside

169

the church. That's the only reason I didn't try and stop her inviting those dreadful stepsisters of hers – because at least they will boost the numbers on our side.'

'Well, I'm *supposed* to be a bridesmaid,' Ava began, 'so I'm not sure if that means—'

But she was interrupted by the fairy godmother letting out an annoyed grunt as she exclaimed, 'Just look at that!'

Ava followed her gaze and saw that Cinderella's stepsisters were standing in the doorway, being announced by the important-looking manservant. Ermentrude was in a very bright, very tight dress that she seemed to be having a lot of trouble walking in and Astrid was in an orange and lime-green ball gown that looked extremely lopsided.

As they watched, a maid directed the

sisters to a table on the other side of the room. The table had a gold banner attached to one end which read: 'COMPETITION ENTRANTS, PLEASE GATHER HERE!'

'They must have decided to enter the dress competition,' the fairy godmother said. 'Well, there's no way either of them will win in those monstrosities, even if they did make the dresses themselves, which I very much doubt! Still – I suppose I shall have to go and test them just the same.'

'Please can I ask you a question first?' Ava said quickly.

'I'm *not* granting any more magic wishes, if that's what you're after,' the godmother said impatiently. 'Honestly! Some people seem to think they can treat me like a genie in a lamp!'

'It's not that,' Ava said at once. 'The

question I've got is about my cat.'

'Your cat?' The fairy godmother looked surprised.

'Yes – she accidentally got into the kitchens the other day and the cook said she gave her to you to practise your spells on. Her name is Cindy and the thing is, I really want her back.'

'Oh, you do, do you?' The fairy godmother paused for a moment. 'I presume you are talking about that very hot-headed female tabby. She's an excellent mouser, so she says.'

'She *is* – unfortunately,' Ava agreed. 'Wait a minute – she actually *told* you that?'

'Oh yes. She also mentioned that at home she is called Cindy – though among other cats she goes by the name of Lucinda Wet-Whiskers the Third.'

'Really?' Ava was astonished. 'So . . . so you understand cat language then?'

'Goodness, no! She told me all this over a nice cup of tea – after I'd changed her into human form.'

Ava gulped.

'Well, perhaps she drank more milk than tea,' the fairy godmother continued, 'but in any case it was all very civilized. Until she smelt my mice, that is, and then she seemed to forget that I had turned her into a human. Clearly my spell needs some refining. Anyway, you can certainly take her away with you if you want. But you'll have to wait until the ball finishes at midnight.'

'Why? Where is she now?' Ava asked.

'The King and Queen were a bit short of staff tonight so I turned your cat into a maid and a couple of the kitchen mice into serving boys. They're all here somewhere. I told the head maid to keep a close eye on them.'

As she talked, she had been walking towards the table where Cinderella's stepsisters were sitting, and Ava had been obliged to walk with her. The ugly sisters were now close enough to recognize Ava, but luckily before they could, the fairy godmother produced a wand from a pocket in her dress and waved it at them.

Ava quickly dodged out of sight as Cinderella's stepsisters screamed, causing all the other guests to turn and stare at them.

Ava couldn't tell at first why they were screaming — until she suddenly realized that the fairy godmother's magic had caused their dresses to vanish. The ugly sisters were standing there, looking totally mortified,

wearing nothing but their
tight corsets and frilly
underclothes.

'Stop that awful noise
and tell me who made
those dresses,' the fairy
godmother commanded,
prodding both girls in
the ribs with the end of
her wand. 'It certainly
wasn't you! I know that
much or they wouldn't
have disappeared!'

Bright red, and staring fearfully at the
wand (which was still giving off some
dangerous-looking sparks), the sisters
answered, 'Our m-m-mother . . . But she's
not very good at sewing . . .'

'I can see that!' The fairy godmother

looked like she was enjoying herself now.

'Well . . . perhaps your punishment should be that you remain at the ball tonight – without any dresses on at all!'

The ugly sisters squealed even louder, and as some of the other guests who had overheard started to laugh and clap at that suggestion, they let out loud sobs and rushed out of the ballroom.

Ava was just wondering whether she ought to follow them and see if they would lead her to wherever they had hidden the music box – after all it might be better not to depend *totally* on her instincts – when she noticed one of the senior maids scolding one of the serving boys. It looked as if he had been caught eating whatever it was he was meant to be serving to the guests from his large silver platter.

'That boy is one of my mice,' the fairy godmother whispered to Ava. 'I hope they haven't given him the cheese straws to hand round. I *told* them what would happen if they did. Oh no! Just look at Cindy over there with the smoked-salmon canapés!'

Ava looked across the room and saw a maid with very strange hair (that could best be described as tabby-coloured) balancing a silver plate of mini pancakes that had smoked salmon on top. Only instead of offering them to the guests, the maid was biting the fish off the top of each one before allowing any of the guests to touch them. Ava watched as she licked her lips, then lifted

177

her fishy fingers to her mouth to lick them clean too.

'Is that girl . . . is that really *Cindy*?' Ava exclaimed, and for a moment she was so fascinated that all she could do was stand and stare.

'Why don't *you* go and speak to her?' the fairy godmother suggested. 'Try and distract her from eating any more of the guests' food. Oh dear,' she murmured, as Cindy put down her tray and started to follow the serving boy who had been eating the cheese straws. 'It was probably unwise to use a mouse and a cat in the same experiment.'

Judging by the way Cindy was now sniffing at the serving boy from behind, Ava assumed the fairy godmother's spell hadn't entirely removed the *smell* of mouse from her subject.

178

'She looks like she's about to tuck into him too,' the fairy godmother said nervously. 'You've got to stop her, Ava. Otherwise there will be a terrible scene and Cinderella's party will be ruined.'

'*Me* stop her?' Ava exclaimed. 'Can't *you* do something?'

But the fairy godmother was already sitting down at the table, where more contestants were arriving to have their dresses tested for authenticity.

That's when Ava knew that it was up to *her* to stop Cindy pouncing on the manservant – or mouse-servant as she reckoned he ought to be called. But how was she going to do it? And besides that, she urgently needed to stop Tilly from coming to the ball and making a complete fool of herself in her borrowed dress. And she *still*

179

had to think of a way of getting the music box back from the ugly sisters . . .

'Cindy, it's me – Ava,' she whispered, gently tapping Cindy-the-maid on the shoulder as she approached her from behind.

The maid whirled round and let out a strange noise that sounded a bit like a purr. 'Ava!' Her voice was like that of a human female, but very throaty. 'What are you doing here?'

'I came to find you and take you home,' Ava said, hardly able to believe she was having an actual conversation with her cat.

'I don't want to come home,' Cindy said in rather a snarly voice, keeping one eye firmly on the serving boy. 'I'm having too much fun.' The boy was now scuttling towards another servant who was holding a tray of cheese vol-au-vents.

'Cindy, I know you won't change back into a cat until midnight, but I really think we should leave the ball *now*. Before you attack that boy and get us both into terrible trouble.'

Cindy-the-maid gave her the same sort of look that Cindy-the-cat gave her when she yelled at her to stop scratching the stair carpet.

'Don't be ridiculous, Ava. I have no intention of attacking anyone. But we have some delicious herring pâté on crackers coming out of the kitchen at any moment. And then I believe we have some prawns. I certainly intend to sink my teeth into some of those!' Cindy started to dribble a little at the thought of yet more fish.

Ava had to think fast. What did Cindy like to eat even more than herring and prawns?

'OK, but first there are some *tuna* sandwiches that need collecting from the kitchen,' she lied.

Cindy's nose started to twitch. Tuna was her favourite fish of all. 'What are we waiting for?' she purred.

Cindy looked so pleased that Ava started to feel guilty at tricking her like this. But as soon as she got Cindy home again she would make up for it by giving her the biggest bowl of tuna she'd ever had.

They were almost at the door when Cindy picked up the scent of the mouse-turned-manservant again – and this time everything happened so fast that there was no time for Ava to stop it.

Cindy's nose twitched again and she let out a strange half-cry, half-growl. Then, shoving two princesses and a duchess out of the way, Cindy hurled herself tiger-like at the other servant. The skinny young man fell to the floor, where he squeaked in fear as Cindy – who had thrown herself down on the ground with him – sank her teeth into his collar and started to drag him towards the door. Despite being the same size as her victim, Cindy seemed to have ten times the strength.

As the surrounding guests screamed, the fairy godmother came rushing over. 'No need to be alarmed, everyone! It's just a little party trick – a little charade we've put on to entertain you!' she trilled.

'Can't you *do* something?' Ava whispered to her as Cindy started to play with her terrified prey, letting him go for a few seconds, then pouncing on him again.

'I'm afraid I can't change either of them back to normal before midnight,' the godmother replied. 'We'll just have to wait until the spell wears off.' She bent down closer to the cat-turned-maid, shouting, 'Do you hear that, Cindy? Let go now and you can eat then if you want.'

As the manservant squeaked even louder, Ava decided that enough was enough. 'Let *go*, Cindy!' she yelled, in much the same stern voice she used whenever Cindy caught a mouse at home.

But Cindy completely ignored her, just as she always did at home, and continued to swat the boy around the head while growling excitedly.

'Get her some more salmon or something!' Ava shouted, but everyone else was backing further away, including the fairy godmother.

'Perhaps I should call the palace doctor –
or the vet,' the godmother was mumbling.
'Oh dear – I don't know which would be
most appropriate . . .'

Desperately Ava grabbed Cindy by the
hair and tugged as hard as she could, and for
a second Cindy loosened her grip on the
manservant for long enough to spit and hiss
at Ava instead. Ava jumped back in fright as
she saw that the maid's fingernails were as
sharp as a cat's claws.

'Get her some FISH somebody!' Ava
yelled again, now on the verge of tears.

Suddenly she heard a familiar voice
calling her name and she looked up to
see a handsome man dressed in a very
princely purple and gold outfit and wearing
a powdered white wig pushing his way
towards her through the crowd of guests.

'DAD!' she exclaimed in amazement.

'Here,' he said, as he reached into his jacket pocket. 'You'd better give this to Cindy before we have our very own fairytale murder to deal with.'

And he pulled out a small can of tuna, with a ring in the lid for easy opening.

Ava watched her dad – with his back to
the rest of the guests – tear off the lid using
the ring pull, then take out a large silk
handkerchief. Carefully shielding the can
from view, he tipped its contents into the
hanky, which he placed on the floor close to
Cindy.

'Cans of tuna don't exist in fairytale land
so we mustn't let anyone see this one,' he
whispered to Ava, slipping the empty tin
back into his pocket.

Thankfully, as soon as Cindy smelt the
tuna she let go of the manservant and

pounced on the fish-filled hanky instead.

'Dad – what are you *doing* here?' Ava asked, as the terrified manservant scrambled to his feet and bolted for the door.

'Rescuing *you*,' her father replied sternly. 'I *told* you things could get dangerous in fairytale land, didn't I?'

'Cindy would never hurt *me*,' Ava said defensively. 'I wanted her to stop attacking that poor little mouse-servant, that's all.'

As she spoke Ava glanced across the room to where there was now a long line of girls in beautiful dresses waiting for the fairy godmother to check them before letting them enter the competition. Ava was relieved to see that Tilly wasn't there yet, but she knew she had to find her immediately to warn her to stay away.

'We can't take Cindy home through

the mirror until the fairy godmother's spell wears off,' her dad continued as they watched Cindy – still on her hands and knees – finishing off the last of the tuna.

'We have to find the music box first!' Ava said anxiously. She started to tell him about the ugly sisters taking the music box for themselves, but he interrupted her.

'I realized something like that must have happened when I arrived through the mirror and found I was inside the wardrobe in their bedroom. Luckily for me they weren't in the room themselves, or I'd have had a lot of explaining to do.'

'Of course!' Ava heaved a sigh of relief as she realized that her father would have to have travelled here the same way she had. Which meant he would have arrived wherever in the palace the music box happened to be. 'Where's the music box now, Dad? You did bring it with you, didn't you?'

He nodded. 'I hid it out in the corridor before I came into the ballroom. We'd better go and fetch it. Then I want you to use it to go straight home, Ava.'

'*No*, Dad!' Ava protested. 'I'm not ready to go back yet. I still have to find Tilly and warn her not to come to the ball. If she does and the fairy godmother totally humiliates her in front of everyone, it will be all my fault!'

'What are you talking about?'

She quickly explained to him what had happened with the competition dresses.

After he had listened to the whole story, her dad sighed. 'Ava, we have to be very careful how we help the people we meet on the other side of the portals. Helping someone by bringing them something from *our* world often *causes* more problems than it solves.'

'I'm sorry, Dad,' Ava said, frowning. 'But *that's* why I need you to take me with you when you go through the portals – so you can teach me what's allowed and what isn't.'

Dad sighed again. 'I think I'm beginning to see that, Ava.'

Ava's heart skipped a beat. 'You *are*?'

'Yes. Now that you know about your gift – however much I wish you didn't – I think I owe it to you to teach you how to use it responsibly. As Marietta says, you're a sensible girl – *most* of the time. Perhaps I just have to trust you more. In any case I intend to explain to you in much more detail how the magic-portal system works – and answer *all* your questions about it.'

Ava tried not to look too excited. After all, she didn't want Dad to think she *wasn't* sensible. But in fact she was so thrilled right at that moment that she felt like dancing about in a way that was totally and utterly crazy!

'So you'll let me stay here long enough to help Tilly?' she asked.

He nodded. 'So long as we keep together.'

Cindy was back on her feet, looking a lot calmer now that she had a full stomach.

'That includes you too, Cindy,' Dad said. 'You need to stay close to us from now on. Come on – I think it's time we left this ball.'

'I'm thirsty,' Cindy complained, eyeing a tray of drinks being carried by a nearby waitress.

192

'It's all that salty tuna, I expect,' Ava said quickly. 'Come with us, Cindy, and we'll soon find you a nice cool drink of water.'

So Cindy accompanied them out of the ballroom into the corridor, where Dad immediately went to retrieve the music box, which he had hidden behind a suit of armour that was on display in a nearby alcove.

'Not the best hiding place, but I was in a bit of a hurry,' he murmured as they set off towards the sewing room – with Ava leading the way and Cindy following in a maid-like fashion a short distance behind them.

Ava decided now would be a good time to ask a question she had been meaning to ask Marietta. 'Dad . . . I've been thinking . . . this isn't the *only* fairytale land we can visit, is it? I mean, there are a lot more fairytales apart from *Cinderella*, aren't there?'

Her father nodded. 'You're beginning to understand how complicated all this is, Ava. Cinderella-land is not the *only* fairytale land in existence, but it's the only one we can visit from Marietta's shop. There are many more shops like Marietta's however – and a lot more magic portals in other places as well.'

'Do you know where all of them are?' Ava asked curiously.

'I know where a lot of them are, yes. For instance, there's a little shop not too far away from where you and your mother live where I go when I want to be transported back to Tudor times. And I've heard they *also* have a portal that takes you to Snow White's cottage.'

'Wow!' Ava exclaimed excitedly. 'Can we go there after this?'

Her father laughed. 'All in good time, Ava.'

'Have you been through *all* the portals in Marietta's shop yet?' Ava wanted to know.

'At one time or another – yes.'

'So when did you last come to Cinderella-land?'

'Oh, it must have been about fifteen years ago or so. I found myself in the middle of a ball the King was throwing for the Queen's birthday. Prince Charming was only a little boy back then, and Cinderella was a very small child living happily in a nearby village with her mother and father.'

Ava was puzzled. 'You mean not everybody comes to Cinderella-land at the time that Cinderella is getting married?'

'Oh, no. It's a bit of a mystery how the fairytale lands work, but they extend a long way, time-wise, on either side of the actual

stories we read about in fairytale books.
You've been exceptionally lucky, Ava,
to arrive here at the most exciting part of
Cinderella's story.'

'I'm *so* glad I did!' Ava gasped. For even
though she wouldn't have minded meeting
Cinderella as a child – or even as an old
woman – the Cinderella she most longed to
meet was the fairytale princess she knew and
loved from her storybook.

Dinah was alone in the sewing room
when they got there, and she immediately
started to struggle to her feet upon seeing
Ava and her father.

'Dinah . . . please . . . you don't have to
curtsy to me,' Ava told the old lady quickly.
'This is my dad, but he's not royalty or
anything, so you don't have to curtsy to him
either.'

'Oh?' Dinah sounded confused – perhaps wondering how Ava could be a princess if her father wasn't a king or a prince. 'I'm very pleased to make your acquaintance, sir,' she murmured, giving him a sort of half-curtsy anyway.

'And I yours, Dinah,' Ava's father replied, bowing his head politely. 'And thank you for helping my daughter.'

'Oh – it was a pleasure, sir.' Dinah looked curiously at Cindy as she lowered herself back on to her chair. 'And I presume this is . . . ?' She trailed off politely as Cindy gave the back of her hand a careful lick to remove a remaining flake of tuna.

'This is Cindy, my cat,' Ava told her. 'The fairy godmother changed her into a maid for the ball. She's not due to change back again until midnight. Do you mind if

197

she stays here until then? Oh, and do you have a drink of water we could give her, please?'

Dinah pointed to a stone jug with two cups sitting on the table. 'There's some water. Does she know how to use a cup?'

'Of course I do, old woman,' Cindy interjected indignantly. 'At the fairy godmother's house I drank milk from a china teacup!'

'Cindy, don't be so rude!' Ava exclaimed, embarrassed.

'It's all right,' Dinah said, trying not to smile. 'Cats aren't the most humble of creatures after all.'

As Dad poured out some water for Cindy, Dinah added in a warning sort of voice to Ava, 'You do realize Cindy might not be quite the same when she changes back again?'

'How do you mean?' Ava asked in surprise.

'Well, the fairy godmother isn't as good at spells as she makes out, you know. This whole glass slipper thing with Cinderella was a mistake, for one thing. I have it on good authority that Cinderella's whole outfit was meant to change back to rags at midnight. Instead, one of her shoes – the one that fell off – stayed as a glass slipper. Of course it all worked out very well for Cinderella in the end, with the prince taking the slipper round to all the houses in the neighbourhood, promising to marry the first girl it fitted! But it wasn't *meant* to happen.' She paused to take a breath. 'So I'm just warning you that when Cindy changes back into a cat, there's a chance that she might not change back *entirely.*'

As Cindy looked alarmed, and Ava looked upset, Ava's dad said quickly, 'Isn't that being rather pessimistic, Dinah? Let's worry about that if it happens, shall we?'

Dinah sniffed. 'Personally I like to be prepared for bad things happening. As I'm always saying to Tilly, at least if you *expect* bad things to happen then you don't get too many nasty shocks.'

'Where *is* Tilly?' Ava asked now.

But Dinah was looking suspiciously at Cindy, who had picked up a freshly mended velvet cape and was rubbing her cheek against it. 'Perhaps it's not such a good idea to keep Cindy in here with all these expensive fabrics,' she told Ava nervously.

'I don't want all my work getting torn – or smelling of fish.'

Ava had to admit she had a point. To make matters worse Cindy was now looking with interest at a small hole in the floor that looked like it could be a mouse hole.

'Is there somewhere else we can take Cindy while we wait for the spell to wear off?' Ava's dad asked Dinah.

Dinah looked puzzled. 'Can't you take her to your guest room, sir?'

Quick as a flash Ava's father replied, 'Of course, but for now I should like her to remain here in the servants' part of the palace. She is a maid, after all.'

'Well . . . you are welcome to take her up to my room, if you want somewhere quiet,' Dinah offered. 'I can show you where it is. I've just been up there helping Tilly get

201

ready for the ball. When I left her she was putting the finishing touches to her hair. Ever so pretty she looked! She should be on her way to the ballroom by now.'

'Oh no!' Ava exclaimed. 'Dad, we have to stop her!'

'Why?' Dinah asked, frowning.

'The fairy godmother is using a special spell to check if the girls entering the competition have made their own dresses or not,' Ava explained to Dinah.

Dinah looked horrified.

'Don't worry. I'll go straight back to the ballroom and fetch her right now,' Ava added, stepping towards the door.

But as she did so, Cindy let out a loud, very *un*maid-like growl of protest.

'Don't worry, Cindy,' Ava said. 'Dad will look after you while I'm gone.'

'Oh no – I'm coming with *you*!' Cindy spat out. 'I don't trust humans who don't like cats.'

Ava stopped in surprise. 'But Dad *does* like cats. Don't you, Dad?'

'Well . . .' Ava's father replied, looking awkward. 'It's not that I *dis*like them, but I suppose, if I'm honest, I *have* always been more of a dog person . . .'

'See what I mean!' Cindy looked disgusted. 'A *dog* person!'

'I tell you what, Ava,' Dad suggested hurriedly as Ava gave him an exasperated look. 'Let's do this the other way round. You and Cindy can stay in Dinah's room, where you'll both be safe – and *I'll* go and fetch Tilly.'

'You can't,' Ava said dismissively. 'You don't even know what she looks like!'

'I'll come with you, sir, after we've taken

Princess Ava and Cindy up to my room,'
Dinah offered at once. 'They won't let me
inside the ballroom, but I can stand in the
doorway and point Tilly out to you.'

'Thank you, Dinah.' Dad was looking at
her gratefully. 'Ava, trust me – it's better
if you stay out of the way of the fairy
godmother. If she finds out that *you* gave
Tilly that dress, who knows what she might
do to you.'

'*I'm* not scared of the fairy godmother,'
Ava said stubbornly.

'Well, you should be,' Dad replied firmly.
'Look what she did to Cindy!'

'Your father is right,' Dinah said. 'It is
safer to stay well away from that woman.
Oh, she *means* well enough most of the
time, but her spells have a habit of going
wrong – sometimes dangerously wrong!

And if she loses her temper there's no telling what she'll do with that wand of hers. She always calms down again afterwards, but by then it's usually too late!'

As Cindy went to lie down for a catnap on one of the narrow beds in Dinah's room, Ava started to look around for a place to temporarily hide the music box. Her dad had slipped it to her when Dinah wasn't looking, and whispered that she should put it somewhere out of sight until he returned. But where?

The room was very small, containing only the two beds, a chest of drawers and two wooden trunks – one at the bottom of each bed. Ava quickly moved the things off the top of the trunk nearest her and opened the lid. The trunk was almost completely full with blankets and various items of clothing that, judging by their size, belonged to Dinah rather than Tilly.

Ava lifted out some folded clothes in order to make some space for the music box. That's when her eye was caught by a brightly coloured piece of fabric sticking out from the folds of one of the blankets at the bottom of the chest. Curiously Ava opened up the blanket and found, hidden inside it, a neatly folded girl's dress. As Ava held up the dress and shook it out, she saw that it was no ordinary item of clothing. It was the most unusual, most perfectly made gown she had ever seen – and it seemed to contain all the colours of the rainbow.

'*This* must be the dress Tilly made for the competition!' Ava exclaimed in amazement. 'But what's it doing *here*?'

12

Ava carefully hid the music box inside the chest and closed the lid, wondering what to do next. She knew that she had to get the dress to Tilly as soon as possible. But how?

The safest option seemed to be to wait here until her dad got back – hopefully with Tilly. After all, if she went off to look for Tilly herself, she might very well miss her and Tilly might arrive back in the servants' quarters while she, Ava, was looking for her at the ball. No, the most sensible thing was definitely to wait.

Ava only hoped there would be enough

time for Tilly to wear her dress to the competition. The dress was so beautiful and so different from all the other dresses Ava had seen in fairytale land that Ava could see now why Tilly thought it had a really good chance of winning. But for that to happen, Tilly had to get here soon.

At last the door opened and Tilly appeared, still wearing the violet and cream dress from Marietta's shop.

'Thank goodness!' Ava said, standing up and sighing with relief.

'Your father came and found me in the queue before I got too near the front,' Tilly said. 'He and Dinah explained about the fairy godmother's spell.'

'That's great, but look!' Ava turned to point at the rainbow-coloured dress, which she had draped over the only chair in the room.

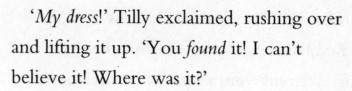

'*My dress!*' Tilly exclaimed, rushing over and lifting it up. 'You *found* it! I can't believe it! Where was it?'

'That's the strange thing. It was . . .' Ava paused, suddenly unsure how to explain *why* she had been looking inside Dinah's wooden trunk. 'I'll tell you later, but shouldn't you hurry up and change, if you're going to wear it to the ball?'

Tilly was beaming with excitement as Ava started to help her out of Marietta's dress. 'I can't believe it!' she kept saying over and over. 'You've got to tell me where it was!'

'I will tell you,' Ava promised. 'But let's wait until Dad and Dinah get here. Where *are* they anyway?'

'Your father is escorting Dinah back to the sewing room. He's a very kind and well-mannered gentleman, isn't he?'

Ava flushed a little as she answered, 'Yes, I suppose he is.' Dad seemed very different here from how he was at home, she thought. In the real world he never seemed to mix much with other people or be very interested in making friends. Here he seemed a lot more *involved* with those around him. In fact, it was almost as if *this* was where he felt most comfortable.

'What do you think?' Tilly asked, after she had carefully pulled on her dress and smoothed down the creases with her hands.

The rainbow-coloured dress appeared to be made of several overlapping layers of fine material. It had a simple, perfectly fitting bodice, long elegant sleeves and a stunning multicoloured sash tied at the waist, beneath which the long flowing skirt billowed out in a mass of rippling colour.

'I've never seen anything like it before!' Ava gasped. For the dress seemed to come alive in an almost magical way as Tilly twirled round, the colours merging with each other like those of a real rainbow.

'Good,' Tilly said grinning. 'Come on. Let's go down to the sewing room and show Dinah.'

Briefly Ava worried about leaving Cindy – who was still asleep on the bed. But she couldn't bear to wake her up and have her cause lots of trouble again. Besides, she reassured herself, in her cat-form Cindy could sleep for hours at a time if she was left undisturbed.

The two girls hurried along the corridor and down the servants' staircase to the sewing room, where Tilly burst into the room excitedly. Ava's father was there with Dinah and when he saw Ava he frowned.

'What are you doing here?' he demanded sternly. 'I told you to wait with Cindy.'

'Cindy's fast asleep, and I'm sure she won't wake up again for ages,' Ava said. 'Dad, I just found Tilly's dress. The one she really *did* make herself! Doesn't she look beautiful in it?'

They were interrupted by an exclamation of concern from Tilly. 'Dinah, what's the matter?'

Both Ava and her father turned to look,

and saw that Dinah had gone very pale. Judging by her face, anyone would think she had just seen a ghost – a *real* ghost – thought Ava.

'Your dress . . .' Dinah murmured, staring at Tilly. 'I'm so sorry . . .'

'It's all right – there's still time to wear it to the ball,' Tilly said, cheerfully. She turned back to Ava and asked breathlessly, 'Where did you find it, Princess Ava? Did the ugly sisters have it?'

Ava slowly shook her head. 'I found it . . . I found it . . .' she began, but something about the look on Dinah's face made her stop.

'It's all right, my dear. Let me tell her,' Dinah said shakily. Slowly she turned to Tilly and continued, 'Princess Ava found your dress in *our* room, Tilly – hidden inside my

213 ✿ ❁ ❀

trunk. The truth is, *I'm* the one who took it.'

'*You?*' Tilly looked disbelieving.

'I was worried about what would happen if you won the competition,' said Dinah. 'To have a wish granted by the fairy godmother seems like such a *risky* prize. You know how unpredictable her spells can be. But it wasn't just that. It was the thought of you going away and leaving me that really made me do it.' Dinah started to cry.

'I don't understand. Why would you think I would leave you?' Tilly asked, still looking incredulous.

'If the fairy godmother grants your wish to have your own dress shop, then of course you'll go,' Dinah replied.

'Don't be silly!' Tilly protested. 'If that happened you could come and work in my dress shop *with* me. I'm not old enough to run a dress shop all by myself in any case.'

Dinah shook her head sadly. 'You'll soon be old enough, Tilly, and by then I probably won't even be able to sew properly any more. I already need your help to thread my needles. The fact is, I'll be worse than useless as a seamstress soon.'

'But, Dinah, I'd want you to come and live with me even if you *couldn't* sew any more!' Tilly exclaimed. 'You're my family, and I would never just go away and leave you! Why would you even *think* that?'

Dinah sniffed. 'Because . . . because . . .' She trailed off, seeming unable to answer.

In the painful silence that followed, Ava's dad said softly, 'Is it because you always expect the worst thing to happen, Dinah?'

Before Dinah could reply, Tilly exclaimed, 'But how could you expect the worst of *me* like that? I'd never just abandon you, after everything you've done for me. I don't know how you could possibly think I would!' She sounded angrier as she added, 'And I don't know how you could be so mean as to steal my dress!'

Dinah hung her head. 'I'm sorry, Tilly,' she said. 'It *was* mean – and I feel terrible about it.'

'No you don't! You wouldn't have said anything if Ava hadn't found the dress. I'll never forgive you for this, Dinah. Never!' And with tears streaming down her face Tilly burst out of the room.

Ava would have gone after her if her dad hadn't put his hand on her shoulder to stop her. 'Leave her for a few minutes, Ava. She needs time to calm down. And I think Dinah has more to tell us.'

He looked questioningly at Dinah who was still looking very pale and teary-eyed.

'What else is there to tell?' Dinah said hoarsely. 'I was afraid, that's all. I've *always* been afraid of losing the people I care about . . . ever since . . . ever since . . .' She broke off.

'Ever since *what*?' Ava asked anxiously.

Dinah sniffed, looking at Ava with a faraway expression in her eyes. 'When I was a small child my parents were so poor they hardly had enough food to feed themselves, let alone me,' she began slowly. 'Nevertheless I loved them and trusted them – just like most children do their parents. One morning they left me on my own to sit and beg by the side of the road. My mother was very tearful that morning but she wouldn't say why. They said if I

217

waited there, they'd come back for me later that day. I started to cry and my father promised that if I was very good they would bring me back a fresh loaf of bread to eat. So I did as they said and I waited. But darkness came and they still hadn't returned. I waited all night for them but they still didn't come. Eventually I realized that they'd abandoned me.' She sniffed again. 'I became a beggar-girl after that and somehow I survived to grow up – but . . . well . . . I suppose I've always been on my guard for bad things happening ever since.'

Ava stared at Dinah speechlessly, hardly able to imagine such a terrible thing happening to a small child. 'Is that why you took Tilly in?' she eventually whispered. 'Because she was left on her own just like you were?'

'Yes, and because I was lonely and I wanted someone to keep me company. Now of course I love her like I would my own daughter. So when she started telling me about her dream to go off and run her own dress shop, I suppose I just panicked.' Dinah's voice was very choked as she added, 'The thing is, Tilly's had just as difficult a start in life as I did. Her parents loved her very much and she missed them terribly after they died. I don't expect her to feel sorry for me – or to forgive me.'

There was a long silence in the room, broken only by the sound of Dinah's weeping.

Ava's dad was looking thoughtful. 'It sounds to me that at least Tilly has always felt *loved* – first by her parents and then by you, Dinah. Perhaps that might help her to forgive you.'

219

As Dinah looked across at him, still crying but with something like a flicker of hope in her eyes, Ava found herself wondering again why she had never seen this side of her dad before.

'Come on, Ava,' Dad added, putting one hand on her arm. 'We have to go and check on Cindy. We'll come back and say goodbye to Dinah before we leave.'

After they had left the room Ava said in a small voice, 'I don't understand, Dad. This is fairytale land, isn't it? I thought that only good things would happen here.'

'Fairytales always end happily for the main characters, like Cinderella and the Prince,' her dad said. 'But some of the other characters don't get quite such a good deal, I'm afraid.'

As he spoke, Tilly stepped out into the corridor from one of the rooms behind them. Her face was still smudged with tears, although she was obviously trying hard to put on a brave face. 'Princess Ava – wait! I want to come to the ball with you!'

Ava and her father both turned, but before Ava could reply her dad said, 'Ava isn't going to the ball, Tilly. But you mustn't let that stop *you*.'

As Tilly's face immediately fell, Ava begged, '*Can't* I go with her, Dad? Please?'

'We can't leave Cindy on her own for any longer,' Dad said firmly. 'And don't ask if I'll stay with Cindy while *you* go to the ball without me, because the answer is no.'

'*I'll* go and sit with Cindy, if it would help, sir,' said a nervous voice – and they looked round to see Dinah standing in the doorway of the sewing room. She still looked pale but she had stopped crying.

'That way you can escort both the girls to the ball. And –' she turned to look timidly at Tilly – 'and afterwards I'd like to try and explain things a bit better to you, Tilly – if you'll hear me out. I know I don't deserve it but . . .' She swallowed.

Tilly frowned uncertainly as she met Dinah's gaze, but after a few moments she slowly nodded.

Ava turned eagerly to her father, who looked like he was weighing up his options.

Eventually he asked Dinah, 'Do you think you can handle Cindy if she turns back into a cat before we return?'

'Oh, I'm sure she'll be *easier* to manage as a cat than as a maid,' Dinah replied. 'Don't worry, sir. I'm perfectly capable of handling her either way.'

Dad turned back to Ava, who was giving

him her most pleading look. 'I suppose there isn't any real danger in letting you go to the ball, so long as I'm with you,' he admitted slowly. 'Since Tilly is no longer wearing the dress you lent her, she shouldn't get into any trouble with the fairy godmother.'

'No – and if she wins the competition, then I *really* want to be there to see it!' Ava said, beaming.

'What time do they announce the winner?' Dad asked Tilly.

'At midnight,' Tilly said. 'Cinderella is to select the winner herself.'

'*Cinderella?!*' Ava gasped. After everything that had happened she had totally forgotten that Cinderella would be at the ball too. And she started to feel light-headed with excitement as she realized that at long last she was going to meet her favourite fairytale princess!

13

The ballroom was packed when they got there. The footman who had been announcing all the guests was still at the door, stifling a yawn and looking grumpy and exhausted. He recognized Tilly and waved her inside impatiently without bothering to announce her, but he clearly expected to formally introduce Ava and her father.

Ava's dad grinned – looking unusually playful all of a sudden as he murmured something to the footman.

'His Royal Highness the Crown Prince

Otto and his daughter, Princess Ava!' the servant boomed out as they entered the ballroom.

Ava gaped in disbelief at her father.

'That's what I called myself when I came here fifteen years ago, so I decided I'd better stick with it,' he told her. Once they were inside the room he seemed to know exactly how to deal with all the other guests, she noticed, as she watched him bow his head politely to an elderly duke and kiss the outstretched hand of his rather haughty-looking, much bejewelled wife.

The ball was now in full swing even though the royal family had yet to arrive. The musicians were playing a fast waltz very energetically, and the couples on the dance floor were whirling round the room – a mass of shimmering colours.

225

Tilly had already gone over to the table where the fairy godmother was sitting. There was only one other young girl left in the queue, waiting to have her dress tested.

Ava waved to her friend, mouthing, 'Good luck!' and Tilly gave her a nervous smile of thanks back.

Ava looked across to where the other contestants were all gathered together waiting for the competition to begin. 'I don't think any of the other dresses are as beautiful as Tilly's, do you?' she said to her father.

'Maybe not, but don't get your hopes up too much, Ava,' he replied warningly. 'We don't know for sure that she'll win.'

'Now you sound exactly like Dinah,' Ava complained, pulling a face.

Dad laughed. 'Oh dear.'

Over at the table, the fairy godmother was already pointing her wand at Tilly and for a few seconds Ava held her breath – but there was no need to worry. Tilly's dress passed the test and she was soon being waved across to stand with the other contestants.

The fairy godmother then raised her hand to signal to the musicians. The music stopped at once and all the guests who had been dancing were asked to leave the floor.

The fairy godmother waited for the dance floor to empty completely before going to stand in the middle of it. 'If I could have your attention, please, lords and ladies, dukes and duchesses, princes and princesses, counts and countesses, earls and . . . hmmm . . . yes . . . well . . . For the next dance I would like *only* the girls in our dress competition to take to the floor. I need to see their dresses

227

more closely before I can decide which six are good enough to make it through to the final – which Cinderella is to judge herself.'

'Where *is* Cinderella?' one of the male guests called out.

'She and the royal family will be here in their own good time, Duke Drink-a-lot,' the fairy godmother replied sharply.

'Yes, well, it's taking them a very *long* time, if you ask me,' muttered the duke grumpily, as he tipped his champagne glass up and downed it in one, before snapping his fingers for a servant to bring him some more.

'He's got a very silly name, hasn't he?' Ava whispered.

Her dad grinned and pointed to a fat man in a gold-trimmed blue velvet suit, who was eating his way through a whole tray full of pork pies. 'That's his friend Earl Eat-a-lot over there. They both looked a lot younger – and a lot slimmer – fifteen years ago.'

Ava giggled as the earl let out a loud burp.

The head footman suddenly stepped into the middle of the floor beside the fairy godmother and cleared his throat loudly. He was holding a scroll of paper in one hand. 'The King has asked me to make some announcements before the royal family make their entrance.' He cleared his throat again before unrolling the paper. 'By royal decree, there is to be no burping or wind-breaking of any description in the presence of the royal family,' he declared, looking pointedly at Earl Eat-a-lot.

This brought an amused titter from the audience and an indignant 'Well, really!' from the earl.

'By royal decree, no one must tread on the toes of any member of the royal household while dancing,' the footman continued.

'I say, do we get thrown into the dungeons if we do?' exclaimed Duke Drink-a-lot jokily – but nobody else laughed.

'By royal decree, no one with bad breath is permitted to dance with their royal highnesses,' the footman added, fixing his gaze firmly on the duke so that nobody could be in any doubt as to who *that* announcement referred to.

The footman went on making announcements, which Ava barely took in because she was so excited. 'I can't *wait* to meet Cinderella,' she whispered to her dad, who was looking at his watch. 'Do you think I'll be allowed to actually *speak* to her?'

But before her dad could reply there was a loud crash as a tray of champagne glasses clattered to the floor just behind them.

'*Mouse!*' a terrified princess shrieked, stamping her feet up and down to try and crush the creature that had disappeared under the long skirt of her gown.

'I say – that servant over there just vanished!' called out another guest in a high-pitched voice. 'Look – those are his clothes!' He was pointing to a pile of servant's clothes on the floor, close to where the tray had fallen.

Other guests started screaming too as
panic quickly spread about the room.

'Dad – *look*!' Ava said, pointing to the
servant who Cindy had attacked earlier.
She had just noticed him standing very still
amid all the activity and his appearance
was changing as they watched.
Grey hair was growing on his
face, and long white whiskers
were growing out from
either side of his mouth.
Two pointy grey ears
were sprouting from the top
of his head, his nose was
turning black and wet, and his
eyes seemed to be shrinking. And
poking out from underneath his
jacket was a very fast-growing tail.

A few seconds later the servant

was gone and in his place was a second heap of clothes and another small squeaky mouse.

'Catch him!' yelled the fairy godmother.

The dress competition was totally forgotten as chaos descended on the ballroom, with the fairy godmother tearing round the room in a frenzy, lifting up the skirts of all the ladies to see if there was a mouse hiding underneath any of them. As all the lady guests shrieked with indignation, their husbands and fathers shouted angrily for the fairy godmother to stop.

In all the commotion, nobody noticed that the footman at the door was trying to make an important announcement. 'Pray be upstanding for His Majesty —' he began, but nobody heard him. 'His Majesty the —' he tried a second time — but still no one was listening.

'*WHAT* is going on here?' a loud voice

suddenly bellowed above the din.

Immediately the whole room froze, for it was the King himself who had spoken.

'For *His Majesty the King*!' the footman finally burst out.

Ava found herself staring in awe at the large man in the glittering crown standing in the doorway as the hushed words, 'Your Majesty,' echoed round the room.

The King nodded regally at his guests as they curtsied and bowed to him, before turning to glower at the fairy godmother, whose face was flushed as she got up from looking under a nearby princess's skirt. 'Well, madam?' he demanded impatiently. 'What is the meaning of this?'

'Your Majesty, there's been a small problem with the servants I brought to help out at the ball,' the fairy godmother replied breathlessly. 'I'm afraid my spell has worn off too soon and they've already turned back into . . . well –' she coughed politely – 'their original forms. It's really most inconvenient and I have to find them straight away.'

'I do believe she's talking about those *mice*,' said an anxious-sounding princess.

'If you ask me, the only good place for mice is cooked inside a pie!' declared Earl Eat-a-lot heartily.

'Hear! Hear!' agreed Duke Drink-a-lot. 'Though a mouse-shake is even better in my opinion!'

'If there are *mice* at this ball, I think I'd rather go home,' exclaimed the nervous duchess standing next to him.

As several of the more panicky guests started to agree with her, the King spoke again.

'There will be no more talk of mice, Fairy
Godmother!' he ordered. 'I will not have
my guests upset like this! You will forget
about your spell and get on with judging
the dress competition. The Queen will be
here shortly with Prince Charming – and of
course Cinderella.'

As he went to sit on the largest of the
throne-like chairs, Ava whispered urgently
to her father, 'Dad, what about Cindy? If
the *mice* have changed back already . . .'

'I was just thinking the same thing,' her
dad replied. 'Dinah's with her of course,
but I still don't think we should stay here
much longer. I'm starting to get rather a bad
feeling about this ball.'

'What do you mean?'

But before he could answer, the fairy
godmother appeared as if from nowhere at

Ava's side. 'Princess Ava – *what* have you done with my maid?' she demanded angrily.

'Cindy's not your maid! She's *my* cat!' Ava protested.

'Maid or cat – I want her back!' the godmother snapped. 'I *must* find out if she has changed back too soon like those wretched mice!'

'We can certainly find that out for you,' Ava's father said quickly, 'if that's all you need to know.'

'Of course it's not *all* I need to know,' the godmother replied, sounding irritated. 'I shall have to conduct further experiments on Cindy to help me perfect my spell. Princess Ava may have her back when – and *only* when – I am finished with her!'

'*If* she's still alive by that time of course – which I seriously doubt!' came a snooty

237

voice from behind them.

Ava turned and gasped in shock as she saw the two ugly sisters standing there. They weren't so much glaring at *her*, Ava realized, as at the fairy godmother.

'What are *you* doing here?' the godmother snapped at them. 'I thought I banished you from the ball!'

They were wearing different ball gowns now, and Astrid was sneering boldly at the fairy godmother as she replied, 'We've spoken to Cinderella about how you humiliated us in front of everybody, and she felt *so* sorry for us that she's given us permission to come tonight after all.'

'Yes – and when she hears about the chaos *you've* just caused, I expect *you'll* be the one banned from the ball – not us!' Ermentrude put in.

Astrid laughed as she continued cattily, 'Even Cinderella is getting tired of the mess you always make with your ridiculous spells! And as for the Queen and Prince Charming – well, they've quite lost patience with you! In fact, they seemed quite interested when we suggested that you be sent away to one of those boarding schools where clumsy fairies are taught to do magic *properly*. The Queen thought you were too old to get a place in such a school, but *we* told her that we know of one that will make an exception for particularly *stupid* fairies!'

Astrid and Ermentrude both burst out laughing, watching gleefully as the fairy godmother's face turned bright red with rage.

'You . . . you . . . wicked girls!' the godmother exclaimed angrily. '*I'll* show you how good my spells are! I shall banish *you* to a boarding school right now – a school on the other side of the kingdom where they specialize in teaching nasty, rude girls better manners!' And before anyone could stop her she was waving her wand high above her head as she shouted out a stream of unintelligible words that seemed to be causing the air around the ugly sisters to sizzle with orange sparks. At the end of her spell she spat dramatically on the end of her wand, at which point there was a loud bang as a cloud of orange smoke totally engulfed the screaming Astrid and Ermentrude.

'Look! They've vanished!' several of the stunned guests exclaimed as the smoke cloud started to clear.

For several seconds nobody spoke. The whole room was staring in amazement at the fairy godmother – who was

still shaking with rage.

Then the silence was broken by a loud, slow clapping. The King had risen to his feet and was actually applauding the fairy godmother. 'Good riddance!' he announced. 'Well done, Fairy Godmother!'

And little by little the whole room started to clap along with the King.

Ava was hugely relieved that the ugly sisters were gone, but suddenly she found herself feeling even more afraid for her cat. 'Dad, we *can't* let her have Cindy back to experiment on her!' she hissed fiercely to her father – but unfortunately the fairy godmother overheard her.

Quick as a flash she turned and pointed her wand at Ava. '*You'll* do as you're told, young lady – unless you want to join Cinderella's sisters.'

'Now, now . . . there's no need for that,'
Ava's father intervened hurriedly. 'You can
have Cindy back if you want her that badly,
Fairy Godmother – of course you can.'
He ignored Ava's protests as he continued,
'But don't you have to judge this dress
competition first? Look – it's already begun.'

The King had just signalled for the music
to start and all the girls whose dresses were
to be judged had started to dance.

The godmother frowned. 'Wait here,' she
ordered them before sweeping across the
room to take her place as competition judge.

'The fairy godmother isn't a totally *good*
character like she is in my fairytale book, is
she, Dad?' Ava said shakily as they watched
her go.

'She's certainly someone you don't want
to get on the wrong side of,' her dad agreed.

'Come on, Ava. We'd better leave now, while she's distracted.'

But Ava had also become distracted by what was happening on the dance floor. In particular she was distracted by Tilly, who was twirling round very fast. Some multicoloured sequins on her dress, which had been barely noticeable before, were now catching the light, and she reminded Ava of a beautiful rainbow sparkling in the sun.

'Can't we just stay long enough to see if the fairy godmother picks Tilly?' Ava begged.

'Ava, there isn't time,' her dad replied firmly. 'If we're still here when the fairy godmother has finished the judging, she'll make us give up Cindy.'

'No, she *won't*,' Ava said defiantly. 'She

can threaten me all she likes, but I still won't tell her where Cindy is!'

'That's very brave, Ava, but the next time she threatens you with her wand, then *I* shall be telling her straight away,' Ava's dad said, taking hold of her hand before she could protest any more. 'Now come with me, please.'

As the fairy godmother requested a temporary halt to the music so that she could shout instructions to the contestants, Ava and her dad began to edge cautiously around the room towards the door. At the open doorway they saw the footman, who seemed to have fallen asleep on his feet. His eyes were shut and he was swaying alarmingly.

As Ava and her dad attempted to slip past him unnoticed, he woke up with a

start, took one look at them, and in his
half-awake state mistook their exit for an
entrance. Even half asleep he clearly had
an excellent memory for names because
he immediately boomed out at the top of
his voice, 'His Royal Highness the Crown
Prince Otto and his daughter, Princess Ava!'

Ava and her father froze as everyone
in the ballroom turned to look in their
direction.

They stayed like that for only a few
seconds. As the furious fairy godmother
raised her wand to point it at them, Ava's
dad clutched her hand more tightly and
shouted, 'RUN!'

14

'Stop!' shouted the fairy godmother, who was very close behind them. 'Stop or I'll turn you both into mice!'

'Keep running,' Ava's dad gasped.

'I'm going to put a spell on your legs to *make* you stop!' the angry godmother yelled, raising her wand just as Ava and her dad came to a place where two of the main palace corridors crossed each other.

Coming down the other corridor towards them, behind an escort of two slow-stepping footmen, was a well-groomed older lady with a crown on her head, dressed in a glittering purple gown. Behind her came a handsomely dressed smiling young man, also wearing a crown, and, on his arm, a beautiful young girl wearing a stunning blue ball gown.

It was the Queen, Prince Charming and Cinderella herself!

'Dad, look! It's Cinderella!' Ava burst out, momentarily forgetting everything else as she strained to get a proper look at her heroine.

'Keep going!' Ava's dad barked, tightening his hold on

247

her wrist as he pulled her across the other corridor directly in front of the royal party.

'Arrest them!' yelled the fairy godmother, waving her wand in a furious manner.

But the footmen had come between the fairy godmother and her targets just as she was pointing her wand. Seconds later the two footmen's legs were completely frozen and they stood rooted to the spot, their arms waving frantically in the air.

The Queen started to scream as Prince Charming shouted angrily at the flustered fairy godmother. Only Cinderella herself remained calm, doing her best to soothe everyone in a soft, sweet voice.

Ava would have loved to stay and meet Cinderella, but of course she couldn't. This might be their only chance to escape – and her dad suddenly seemed to have a good

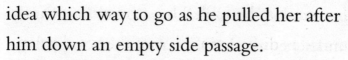

idea which way to go as he pulled her after him down an empty side passage.

Thankfully they managed to find their way to the servants' quarters – after stopping briefly to ask a surprised maid for directions – and once they got there, Ava quickly found the right door.

Inside the little room, Dinah was sitting on her bed with Cindy on her lap.

'Thank goodness!' Ava gasped, running over to pick up her beloved cat, who purred loudly as she started to stroke her. 'Is she all right? There aren't any bits of her that haven't changed back, are there?'

'None that I can see,' said Dinah. 'I got a bit of a shock when it happened, though. I thought she wasn't going to change back until midnight!'

'Something went wrong with the fairy

godmother's spell,' Ava said, tickling Cindy under her chin. 'Oh, Cindy, I'm so glad you're a cat again!'

'She's certainly much *nicer* as a cat,' Dinah agreed. 'So . . .' She looked a little anxious now. 'How is Tilly? How is she doing in the competition?'

'We're not sure. The competition hasn't really got started properly,' Ava told her.

'The fairy godmother has been chasing after *us*, instead of getting on with the judging,' Dad explained. 'She's trying to force us to give her Cindy so that she can discover what went wrong with the timing of her spell.'

'I *told* you her spells hardly ever go according to plan,' Dinah grunted. 'I always make sure I steer well clear of her whenever she waves that wand of hers – and I wish Tilly would too!'

'She just did a very *successful* spell on the two ugly sisters,' Ava pointed out, but before she could explain further her father cut in.

'*We* need to steer well clear of her from now on too, Dinah – which means we have to leave immediately!'

Dinah looked him straight in the eyes. 'I expect you'll be needing your music box then.'

Ava gasped out loud, while her dad was momentarily speechless.

'I couldn't understand what made you open up my wooden chest, Ava,' Dinah continued. 'So I had a look inside myself, and I found that you'd been in there for a reason that had nothing to do with Tilly's dress.'

Ava flushed as her dad said quickly, 'It's not how it looks, Dinah. Ava wasn't trying to *steal* the music box. It's just that—'

But Dinah swiftly raised a hand to silence

him. 'Don't worry. You don't have to explain.' She paused. 'You see, a long time ago – twelve years or so, I'd say – there was another girl who came here pretending to be a princess. *She* needed the music box to get home too.'

'*What* other girl?' Ava blurted, glancing sideways at her dad, who had suddenly become very still.

'She called herself a *travelling* girl,' Dinah continued. 'She was quite a bit older than you – sixteen or thereabouts. Very pretty, she was, with long reddish hair. She was rather an angry, mixed-up sort of girl, but I understood why. You see, just like me, she had been abandoned by her parents.'

Ava's mouth fell open and she looked questioningly at her dad. Could it be . . . ?

'She wouldn't tell me where she came

from or anything about the magic she used to get from place to place,' Dinah went on. 'But she did say that she was running away from home – from an older brother she didn't get on with. He was very bossy and overprotective, she said – always fussing about where she was and what she was doing. But he was her only family since their parents had left them – and I told her she was lucky to have him. I was alone in the world at the time, you see, so I knew what it was like to be completely without family. It was before I adopted Tilly.'

There was a short silence. Ava glanced at her dad and was taken aback to see tears in his eyes.

Without looking at Ava, her father murmured quietly, 'I'm very grateful to you for helping her, Dinah.'

'I thought you might be related to her

when I found the music box,' Dinah said.
'You're her brother, aren't you?'

Silently he nodded.

Dinah smiled in a knowing sort of way.
'I've heard a lot about you over the years.'

'You have?'

'Oh yes. Marietta has become quite a
frequent visitor. After all, we have a lot
in common, both being dressmakers. I'm
surprised that she hasn't mentioned me
before now . . .'

'Yes, well . . .' Ava's dad grunted. 'Marietta
makes it a rule to tell me very little about
her travels. She says she's afraid I'll *interfere* if
I know too much. Where she gets *that* idea
from, I don't know . . .'

Dinah was trying not to smile. 'She did
mention something about you disapproving
of some of her friends in the past – and that

she'd felt rather embarrassed when you made
it your business to tell them so! Anyway,' she
added hastily, 'it will be absolutely *lovely* to
see her tomorrow at Cinderella's wedding!'

'*Marietta's* coming to the wedding?' Ava
exclaimed in surprise.

'Oh yes. She's made herself a very
beautiful new dress to wear, I believe.'

Ava immediately remembered the raspberry-
coloured gown she had seen hanging up in
Marietta's shop, but before she could tell Dinah
about it her dad was continuing in an urgent
voice, 'Dinah, about this music box . . .'

'Oh, don't worry about that. *I'll* take it
back to the music room after you've gone,'
Dinah offered at once. 'I've done that many
a time for your sister.'

'Are you sure? I don't want to get you
into any trouble.'

'Oh, I won't get into trouble. If anyone sees me with it, I'll just say that some guests borrowed it and asked me to return it for them,' Dinah said.

'But, Dad, we *are* coming back here tomorrow for Cinderella's wedding, aren't we?' Ava asked anxiously, watching her father open Dinah's wooden chest and take out the music box. 'I still have to meet Cinderella properly! And I'm to be a *bridesmaid* at her wedding, remember!'

'Ava, we can't risk another encounter with the fairy godmother,' he said. 'I'm sorry. Marietta can do what she likes of course, but it's not safe for *you* to go to Cinderella's wedding now.'

'But, Dad, that's not fair!'

'It's the way it has to be, I'm afraid, Ava,' her father said firmly.

'But I don't want to go home yet!' Ava's lower lip trembled and tears pricked her eyes.

'Ava, it won't take long for the fairy godmother to find that maid who gave us directions. Then she'll know we were heading for the servants' quarters. And if she catches us here, not only will she take Cindy and do goodness knows what to her, but Dinah will be in big trouble for helping us. That's not what you want, is it?'

Ava sniffed. 'Of course not, but—'

'Good – now listen carefully.' He opened the music box. 'You go first, with Cindy. I'd take her myself but I think she'll be calmer with you. And I'll be following right behind you so don't worry.'

'Don't forget these, Ava,' Dinah suddenly said, holding out the dress and shoes Ava had lent Tilly from Marietta's shop. Dinah

257

had a thoughtful look on her face as she handed over the dress – stroking the silk violets on the skirt as if they had given her an idea – but whatever she was thinking, she didn't say anything.

As Ava took her position in front of the music box with Cindy she was struggling not to cry. 'Will you say goodbye to Tilly for me, Dinah?' she said miserably. 'Tell her I hope she wins the competition!'

Dinah gave her a hug. 'I'll tell her – and don't be too disappointed about having to go home, my dear. After all – you never know when something good may be just around the corner.'

This was so unlike Dinah that for a moment Ava stared at her in surprise, wondering if the fairy godmother had cast some sort of spell on *her* – one that had

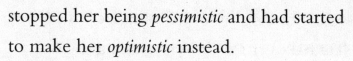

stopped her being *pessimistic* and had started
to make her *optimistic* instead.

Then Ava's dad was ordering her to look
in the mirror and concentrate . . .

Feeling as if she hadn't fully returned yet
to the real world, Ava sat quietly on the
floor in the upstairs room of Marietta's
shop – with Cindy curled up in her lap –
waiting for her father to arrive through the
mirror. When he didn't appear after another
few minutes, Ava started to worry, and
decided to go and find Marietta.

'You're back!' Marietta exclaimed in
delight when she saw Ava. 'And Cindy too!
Wonderful!'

As Marietta spoke, Cindy jumped out
of Ava's arms on to the settee, where she
settled herself against a cushion, lazily licking

her paws as if she was cleaning them after an everyday trip out into the back garden.

'*She* doesn't seem any the worse for her travels, in any case,' Marietta said, smiling as she turned to Ava. 'So what about you? Did you have a good time?'

'Yes,' Ava replied, 'but I'm worried about Dad. He was supposed to be following me back through the mirror straight away.'

'Oh, I shouldn't worry about *him*,' Marietta said reassuringly. 'Otto can usually take care of himself – *and* everybody else! He's rescued me out of a few scrapes in my time, I can tell you. Now, tell me about your visit. Did you meet Cinderella?'

'Not properly – but we met Dinah and Tilly,' Ava said.

'Really?' Marietta looked momentarily taken aback. 'Your father met Dinah too?'

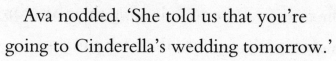

Ava nodded. 'She told us that you're going to Cinderella's wedding tomorrow.'

'That's right. Isn't it exciting? I've been waiting years for it to happen – and now you and I can go together!'

Ava shook her head sadly. 'Dad won't let me.'

'Why ever not?'

Ava was about to explain when they heard footsteps above them, and seconds later Dad appeared on the spiral staircase.

'Dad, I'm so glad you're back!' Ava cried out, rushing to give him a hug.

'Ava was getting worried about you,' Marietta told him lightly when he looked surprised.

'Really?' Ava's dad stroked her hair a little awkwardly as he explained, 'I'm sorry, Ava. I stayed behind for a bit longer because

261

Dinah wanted to discuss an idea she thought might interest us.'

'What idea?' Ava asked curiously.

But before he could answer Marietta said in a rush, 'So, Otto . . . you've met Dinah?'

'Yes, Marietta, we have,' he replied crisply. 'And I gather she's known *you* since you were a teenager.' He was giving his younger sister rather a stern look, considering she hadn't actually *been* a teenager for quite some time, Ava thought.

Marietta laughed, a little self-consciously. 'She told you about when we first met?'

'She certainly did.'

'Ah, well . . .' Marietta sighed. 'It was a very long time ago, Otto. I was young and headstrong and I didn't like being bossed about by my ultra-sensible older brother!'

'I did *not* boss you about,' Ava's dad said, sounding irritated.

'You wouldn't let me leave school and go off travelling like I wanted to,' Marietta pointed out.

'You were too young to drop out of school! Anyway, *someone* had to give you some guidance – and it wasn't as if our parents were there to do it!'

'I know that, Otto,' Marietta said. 'And I'm very grateful to you for trying so hard to take their place – really I am.' She spoke sincerely, though she also had a twinkle in her eye. Turning to Ava, she added, 'I was a bit of a wild child when I was younger, Ava. Your dad was always looking out for me and stopping me getting into *too* much trouble.'

As Ava looked at them both she suddenly felt that there was much more she wanted to ask them about their lives when they were young – and about her missing grandparents.

But right now the thing she was most interested in was what Dinah had just said to Dad that sounded like it involved *her*. 'So what *was* Dinah's idea, Dad?' she prompted him.

Her father turned to look at her. 'Dinah's idea? Ah, yes . . . well . . . Dinah knows how much you were looking forward to being one of Cinderella's bridesmaids, but she agrees with me that it's too dangerous as things are at the moment. The ugly sisters may be out of the way but there's still the fairy godmother to consider. However, she has another idea. Apparently the fairy godmother has one weakness – flowers!'

'Flowers?' Ava was puzzled.

'Yes. According to Dinah, not only do flowers make the fairy godmother sneeze, but she is quite unable to perform any magic on a person who is carrying more than a hundred of them.'

'A *hundred*!'

'Yes – it's all to do with some flower spell she once did that went badly wrong. Anyway, what Dinah suggested is that rather than going to Cinderella's wedding as her bridesmaid, you should go as her flower girl instead. What do you think?'

'Great! But how will I hold that many flowers?'

'Oh, you don't have to *hold* all of them,' Dad replied, smiling. 'Does she, Marietta?'

'Of course not,' Marietta said, smiling too. 'All we need to do is find the right flower-girl dress for you to wear, Ava – and I believe I have just the one! Come on! Let's go upstairs and you can try it on right now!'

15

'So what do you think?' Ava asked her dad the next morning as she pushed back the sparkly curtain of the changing cubicle and gave a little twirl.

'You look beautiful,' he declared, smiling proudly.

Ava's flower-girl dress was made of very swishy cream silk, on to which dozens of pretty silk flowers of all different colours were sewn. On her feet she wore sandals that were also totally covered with silk flowers, and on her head was an elegant headband that had beautiful silk daisies sewn on to it.

'I can hardly believe they're going to turn into real flowers when I go through the portal!' Ava exclaimed. 'Marietta says she used a very special type of magic thread to sew them on. Look – you can actually see it sparkling.'

Dad glanced at the thread she was pointing to and nodded matter-of-factly. 'Has Marietta checked that you have *enough* flowers?' he wanted to know.

'She says when I get my flower basket I'll have well over a hundred, so I'll be quite safe,' Ava reassured him. She frowned slightly because there was something she wanted to ask and she wasn't sure how Dad would react. 'Dad, I've brought my camera with me . . . and . . . well . . . do you think you could take a photograph of me in this dress so I can show Mum? It's just that I really wish she could be here to see it too.'

'Of course we can take a picture,' Dad said at once. 'As long as—'

'As long as I don't tell her where I got the dress,' Ava finished for him. 'Don't worry. I know I mustn't say anything about Marietta's shop.'

As she spoke, Marietta came down the spiral staircase to join them. She was wearing the raspberry-coloured fairytale gown that she had modelled on the music-box princess's. It had a snug-fitting bodice and a massive skirt, which swayed regally when she walked. She had a sparkling tiara in her hair and a matching necklace around her neck. On her feet she wore shoes made of raspberry-coloured glass, each of which had a glass rosebud on the front that matched the silk rosebuds decorating her dress.

'I believe glass slippers are the "in" thing now in fairytale land,' she told them, smiling. 'I must say they are not the most comfortable of shoes, so goodness knows how I shall dance in them – but they do look stunning!'

'*You* look stunning,' Ava's father said warmly. 'Now promise me, both of you, that you'll be careful while you're away. I'd come with you, except that I don't think the fairy godmother would be very pleased to see me. Besides –

269 ❀❀❀

weddings aren't really my thing!'

'We promise,' Ava said, smiling.

'So long as *you* promise to be polite to my customers, if there are any while I'm gone, Otto,' Marietta added as she pulled on a pair of cream silk gloves.

Dad laughed. 'I'll do my best. And I'll *also* do my best not to lose Cindy again while you're away. Now, if you fetch your camera, Ava, I'll take that photo you wanted. Then I think you two princesses had better get a move on, if you don't want to be late for the big event!'

Ava arrived on the other side of the mirror to find herself not in the palace music room, as she'd expected, but outside in the royal gardens. Marietta, who had travelled through the magic portal first, was standing

on the grass waiting for her, her red hair glinting in the sunshine.

'Look at my dress!' Ava exclaimed. The silk flowers that had decorated it before had magically blossomed into beautiful, sweet-smelling real ones.

Before Marietta could reply, a familiar voice behind Ava called out, 'Wow! You look really . . . *flowery!*'

Ava turned to see Tilly in her rainbow-coloured dress, beaming at her. The palace music box was sitting on the grass at her feet, glowing slightly.

'Tilly!' she exclaimed, delighted to see her friend.

'I won the competition!' Tilly told her breathlessly. 'And it's all thanks to you, Ava, for finding my dress!'

As the two girls hugged, Tilly added, 'And

guess what? Since the fairy godmother's spells have been going a bit wrong lately, Cinderella suggested I choose a different prize. Dinah told me about the music box and why it was so special, so I asked Cinderella if I could have that and she said yes! We're going to keep it in the sewing room, so you and Marietta can come and visit us whenever you like without worrying about running into the fairy godmother. *Or* the ugly sisters – if they ever come back here, that is!'

'That's great, Tilly – but what about your dress shop?' Ava asked in surprise.

'Well, Cinderella likes the dress I made so much that she's asked me to be her personal dressmaker after she marries the prince. Then, when I'm older, she's going to help me get set up in my own shop, with a little flat above it for me and Dinah to live in.'

'So you and Dinah are friends again?'

Tilly nodded. 'I know Dinah's really sorry for taking my dress, and it's difficult to stay angry with her after everything she's done for me.'

'Girls, I know you have a lot to catch up on, but we mustn't forget we have a wedding to go to,' Marietta interrupted them now. 'I've waited all this time for Cinderella to get married – and I don't want to miss it!'

'Don't worry. It's not due to start for another half an hour, over there in the big walled garden,' Tilly said, pointing to the far side of the lawn, where they could see a high brick wall with a door set into it. The door had been propped open and servants were hurrying in and out, carrying cushions and extra chairs.

'I thought the fairy godmother said the

273

wedding was to be in a church,' Ava said.

'It was, but at the last minute Cinderella and Prince Charming decided it should be outside in the open air instead. Come on. I'll show you,' Tilly said.

Marietta and Ava followed Tilly towards the walled garden. As they got closer they could hear the sound of lots of people chattering.

'Wow!' Ava gasped as they reached the door and looked in.

The walled garden had been turned into a very beautiful open-air room. The guests were seated in rows on either side of a red carpet that had been placed down the centre to create an aisle. Where the carpet ended there was an archway with beautiful flowers laced through it – under which the young couple would take their marriage vows. The

four walls of the garden were covered in
rambling pastel-coloured roses, which gave
off a very sweet scent.

'The fairy godmother was very cross
about all the flowers – but Cinderella
insisted,' Tilly said, grinning.

Along the tops of the walls, small animals

had started to gather. Ava saw red squirrels, grey rabbits, white doves, three baby owls with their mother, a robin (even though it was summertime) and some lively fox cubs who were being miaowed at to sit still by a cross mother cat who was there with her four kittens.

'Cinderella has befriended a lot of the animals who live in the palace grounds,' Tilly explained. 'And they all want to see her get married. She's even having a choir of bluebirds perform – they're just tuning up down in the vegetable garden.'

'Hadn't you better go and join the bridal party now, Ava?' Marietta said.

'I'll take you,' Tilly offered at once. 'Dinah is with them and she'll give you your flower basket.'

'Tell Dinah that I'm looking forward to

catching up with her after the wedding,'
Marietta said.

'I'll tell her,' Tilly replied. 'Come on,
Ava. But watch out for the fairy godmother!
She's in the garden somewhere too,
practising her confetti spell. She wants to
make confetti fall out of the sky immediately
after the wedding ceremony – but every
time she tries it, she makes it pour with rain
or start snowing instead!'

Ava followed her friend across the grass to
the palace – thankfully *without* encountering
the fairy godmother – and into a huge light
room which had glass doors along one side
that opened out on to the palace gardens.

Inside, Dinah was ordering the excited
bridesmaids to stand still as she gave their
dresses a final inspection. 'Oh, there you are,
Tilly! And Princess Ava is with you! How

lovely!' She came over to Ava and gave her a kiss on the cheek. 'You look beautiful, my dear . . .' she said, adding in a low voice, 'Now, there's nothing to worry about. I've already told Cinderella that you're going to be her flower girl, and your flower basket should be arriving at any minute.'

'Where *is* Cinderella?' Ava asked eagerly, looking around the bustling room and seeing no sign of the bride.

'She said she needed to get some fresh air,' Dinah told her.

'I bet I know where she is,' Tilly said. 'Come on, Ava.'

Tilly led Ava through the glass doors out into the garden. 'There's a spot on the other side of that bush where Cinderella often goes when she wants to be on her own,' Tilly told her, pointing at an extremely large bush with big orange flowers growing all over it. 'Why don't you see if she's there now?'

So Ava left Tilly and headed across the grass, her heart pounding.

'Oh!' she gasped excitedly, because standing on the other side of the bush, gazing dreamily into the distance, was Cinderella herself, looking just like she had stepped out of a fairytale book.

The full skirt of her wedding dress was made from several layers of crushed

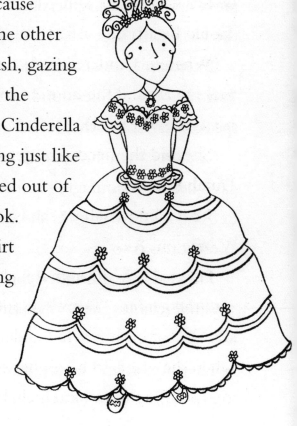

white silk draped over a hooped underskirt. The bodice was also white silk, with dainty little flowers embroidered on to it. On her feet Cinderella wore what looked like her original glass slippers. Her golden hair was piled up high on her head and decorated at the back with tiny white jasmine flowers.

'Excuse me,' Ava began in a shy whisper, 'but . . . but . . .' She found herself unable to speak because her throat had gone so dry.

Cinderella saw how nervous she was and gave her an encouraging smile. 'You must be Ava, my flower girl,' she said sweetly. 'Your dress is so . . . so . . .'

'Flowery?' Ava finished for her.

Cinderella laughed. 'Yes. But very pretty too.'

Then Ava found herself gushing, 'Cinderella, I've been wanting to meet you for ages! You're my favourite of all the fairytale princesses! And you must be *so* excited about marrying Prince Charming! He's *very* handsome, isn't he?'

'You are very kind,' Cinderella replied graciously. 'And yes, I am looking forward to marrying Prince Charming very much. He is the sweetest person I have ever met – even if he does get a little flustered by the antics of my godmother!' She frowned slightly. 'But I must confess, Ava, that I am rather anxious about the wedding itself. I only hope I don't let everybody down. There will be so many people there looking at me. What if I get so nervous that I can't speak? Or what if I trip up on my way down the aisle – or do something else silly that will make everyone laugh at me?'

'Cinderella!' Dinah's voice called out

urgently, making them both jump. 'It's nearly time to go!'

'You mustn't worry,' Ava reassured her heroine earnestly. '*You* could never do *anything* that would make people laugh at you. You're *Cinderella*!'

Cinderella sighed. 'The thing is, Ava, I'm just an ordinary girl really, underneath all these fancy clothes.'

'Cinderella, you will *never* be ordinary!' Ava told her firmly.

And neither will I, Ava thought to herself as she accompanied Cinderella back across the garden to the palace. For now that she had discovered Marietta's shop, and with it the amazing truth about her dad – and about herself – Ava knew that her life was going to be anything *but* ordinary from now on!